Samantha and the Detective

By Paige Tyler

Published by Blushing Books ®,
a subsidiary of
ABCD Graphics and Design
977 Seminole Trail #233
Charlottesville, VA 22901

The trademark Blushing Books ® is registered in the US Patent and Trademark Office.

Paige Tyler
        Samantha and the Detective
ISBN 978-1-935152-18-7

Cover Design: Rae Monet

Thank you for purchasing this copy of title by Author

Please check out our websites sites, including Spanking Romance, located at http://www.spankingromance.com. A completed novel or novella is published here each week.

We also operate Bethany's Woodshed, located at (http://www.herwoodshed.com) the Internet's oldest and largest spanking story site. In operation since 1998, Bethany's has published hundreds of full length spanking romances, all professionally written. Please check out our website for more wonderful stories by Author and other fine authors.

We also run an eBook site at Romantic Spankings (http://www.romanticspankings.com). Here you will find hundreds of eBooks for immediate download.

Our print book site is located at SpankBooks. (http://www.spankbooks.com)

Paige Tyler is a full-time writer of erotic romance. She and her research assistant (otherwise known as her husband) live on the beautiful Florida coast. For more of her sexy erotic fiction visit

www.paigetylertheauthor.com

Chapter One

It was only ten-thirty in the morning and it had already been a long day. But that was because Hayden Tanner had been up since four AM when he'd been called down to the university after some early morning joggers had found the body of a fellow student dumped beside one of the fitness trails. A half dozen members of the track club had been getting in some cross-country work before class and had seen a bare leg sticking out of some shrubs.

From the looks of it, the naked body had been tossed from a car parked on the road up the hill from the trail. There were cuts, scrapes, and bruises on the body that the ME had said were post mortem, which fit with the theory that the body had been dumped after the murder. Preliminary cause of death was strangulation since there were heavy ligature marks around the man's neck.

The combination of the naked body, rope marks on the wrists, and the college campus dumpsite gave the murder all the indicators of a sex crime, but Hayden was reserving judgment until he and his partner got the results from the autopsy. At least one thing was sure, though; they could definitely rule out suicide.

As it happened, one of the joggers had recognized the vic and identified him as an art major that had a part-time job at one of Seattle's small bookstores, which was where Hayden and his partner were now.

"So, when did you say you saw him last?" Hayden asked the store's owner.

The man was well past middle age, with a thin, angular face and wire-rimmed glasses that hid unremarkable gray eyes. He was just the type of man that Hayden would imagine owning a bookstore.

Before the man could answer his question, however, the door to the shop opened. Hayden turned to find a woman entering the store. She was young, probably no more than twenty-five or so, and pretty, with ash blonde hair that she had loosely pulled up into a clip and sunglasses perched atop her head. She was petite, too, he noticed. In fact, if not for the stacked heels she was wearing, she'd probably barely reach his chin.

But it was her eyes that fascinated him. They were the clear, blue-green color of the Caribbean. And, no doubt, just as easy for a man to drown in.

Her gaze immediately locked on the badges he and his partner wore, and she hurried over to them eagerly.

"What are you doing here?" she asked even as her blue eyes took on a knowing look. Slipping on a pair of reading glasses, she took a spiral notebook out of her handbag. "This must be about Rick Elliot, right?"

Hayden's eyes narrowed. Damn, she was a reporter. He should have known. "And how do you know about that?" he asked crossly.

She barely spared him a glance as she fished a pen out of her huge shoulder bag. "My scanner," she said, as if that should have been obvious. "What happened?"

Hayden's dark brows drew together. With a quick look at his partner, who was regarding him with amusement, he abandoned his questioning and took her arm. "I'm Detective Hayden Tanner and since this is a police investigation, I'll be the one asking the questions. In fact, I think I have a few for you," he said, hustling her out the door.

"Let go of me! I'm sure even a Neanderthal like you has heard of the First Amendment. I have every right to be here." Samantha Halliwell wrenched her arm from the detective's grasp once they were outside and glared up at him. "Who taught you manners? The Marquis de Sade?"

His mouth twitched in wry amusement at her quip. "Who?"

"Forget it!" she snapped. "I'm sure it's above you."

His jaw tightened slightly at the insult. "Who are you?" he asked. "I've never seen you around a crime scene before."

Samantha was glad she'd worn her chunky sandals. Even with them, she barely came up to his chin, and she lifted hers defiantly. "Samantha Halliwell from the Post."

Gold eyes narrowed and his voice took on an accusing tone. "I never heard of you."

Samantha looked up at the handsome man before her. He would have been what her younger sister called "a hottie" if he weren't so damn arrogant, which was why she wasn't the least bit affected by his broad shoulders, rugged good looks, or incredible amber-colored eyes. "And you know all the reporters that work for the Post?"

He lifted a brow. "Just the good ones."

She flushed and looked away. "I work in the arts and leisure section," she said softly.

The detective had to bend his head to hear her words. "The what?"

Her gaze snapped back to his. "Arts and leisure," she said stiffly, louder this time and carefully punctuating each word.

To her surprise – and intense irritation – he burst out laughing. "What? You're not even a real reporter!"

"I am too, you jerk!" How dare he say that to her! Just because she wrote about gallery openings and movies didn't mean she wasn't a real reporter. "So, what can you tell me about Rick Elliot's murder? Do you think Jack Kendall was involved?" she asked, referring to the dour faced man who owned the bookstore.

Hayden Tanner's mouth tightened. "If you were a real reporter, you would know that one, Rick Elliot's death has not been officially ruled a murder and won't be until the final autopsy report comes in, and two, I wouldn't be able to comment on who might or might not be involved."

She folded her arms and gave him a contemptuous look. "Oh, please! His naked body was found with rope marks around his neck. What did he do – stumble and choke himself on a tree limb while out jogging in the nude?"

"Where did you get that information?" he demanded.

She smiled sweetly at him. "Anonymous source. Are you confirming the cause of death, then?"

He scowled. "No comment."

She sighed. "Come on, give me something I can use. What's Kendall got to do with this?"

"No comment."

"How typical!"

"Look, there's no story here, so why don't you run back to your desk at the Post." He smirked. "I'm sure there's some new movie out needing a bad review or something."

Her hand itched to slap that sardonic smirk off his smug face. Lifting her chin, she secured her bag more firmly on her shoulder and gave him a scathing look. "If you'll excuse me, I need to ask Mr. Kendall some questions."

She made as if to push past him, but he caught her arm. "I don't think so, Ms. Halliwell. Not unless you want me to arrest you for interfering in a police investigation." His mouth quirked. "Though the idea of you in a pair of handcuffs does hold a certain appeal."

Samantha simply stared at him, speechless and blushing as something warm and tingling coiled its way around her. Surprised by her reaction, she quickly tucked a strand of hair behind her ear and made a show of putting her notebook back into her bag.

"Tell Mr. Kendall that I'll be back to talk to him," she said, trying to maintain as much of her dignity as she could.

This time, Hayden let her go. But as his gaze followed her down the street, he felt himself grow hard, and he swore under his breath. What the hell was the matter with him? She was a reporter and he hated reporters, even beautiful reporters with incredibly blue eyes and the sexiest ass he'd ever seen.

8

Swearing under his breath again, Hayden went back inside. His partner, Nik, was just finishing up with Jack Kendall and filled Hayden in as they walked back to the car. The bookstore owner hadn't been able to tell them anything useful, not that Hayden thought he would. Having been a college student once himself, Hayden doubted that Rick Elliot would have confided in his employer about his personal life. The age difference, if nothing else would prevent that.

"So, what's the deal with that reporter?" Nik asked as Hayden pulled out onto the street.

Hayden scowled. He didn't want to talk about Samantha Halliwell. He paused in mid-thought, surprised that he had actually remembered her name. "What's the deal with any reporter?" he said bitterly. "They want a story. Even if they have to make it up."

Nik shrugged. "I suppose," he agreed. "But you gotta admit that she was hotter than most reporters we know."

"I didn't notice," Hayden muttered.

His partner laughed. "Sure you didn't."

Hayden clenched his jaw, but said nothing. Nik knew him too well for him to try and deny it. Not that it mattered, he thought. Samantha Halliwell was a reporter and he didn't get involved with reporters. Not anymore.

"You know," Nik said quietly. "Every reporter isn't like Jessica."

"How would you know?" he asked angrily.

Nik held up his hands. "I'm just saying."

Hayden's hand tightened on the steering wheel. He had met Jessica Riley a few years ago when she'd been doing a story on a case he was working. He had been younger then and a hell of a lot more inexperienced, at least when it came to women – women reporters, in particular. In the beginning, Jessica's questions about the case had been innocent enough, and because he had been half in love with her, he had trusted her, especially when she had assured him that everything he'd told her would be off the record.

It wasn't.

Everything he'd told her had ended up being front-page news, which had not only jeopardized the investigation, but had also almost cost him his career. And the worst part was that she had laughed in his face when he had confronted her about it. He wouldn't be so foolish again.

Detective Hayden Tanner had struck a chord when he'd told Samantha that she wasn't a real reporter. She had been editor of her college newspaper, gotten an internship with the Post between her junior and senior years, and had graduated cum laude with a degree in journalism. She was most definitely a real reporter.

While most journalism students were lucky if they got a job working at some tabloid after they'd graduated, she had been fortunate to have been hired by one of the top papers. She simply didn't want to work in the arts and leisure section of that paper forever. Which was why she had begged the editor to let her run with the Rick Elliot story. She was lucky he had a few of his most trusted reporters out sick with some bug, otherwise he would never have used her on a story as big as a murder at the university. She knew she had to get a lead quick or he'd replace her with a more seasoned reporter they got over whatever it was that they had.

But there wouldn't be any story if Detective Tanner had anything to say about it, she thought morosely. What was up with that jerk anyway? she wondered, watching from her car as he and his blond-haired partner left the bookstore. It wasn't like she was going to interfere with the investigation. She would simply follow the case and talk to the necessary people to get her story.

Of course, it would be nice if Detective Tanner would toss her a bone. Almost every investigative reporter on the Post had told her that the best way to get an inside scoop on any story was to make a friend of the lead detective on the case. She could do worse than Detective Tanner, she reflected, thinking of the tall, handsome cop. He was definitely easy on the eye. Pity he didn't have the personality to match.

10

She thought a moment. Perhaps there was a way to get in good with him. Like if she were to learn something in the course of her investigation of Rick Elliot's murder, something that the good detective hadn't managed to uncover, and then offer it up to him in return for some information... That had potential, she thought.

Samantha waited for the detectives to leave before she made her way across the street and back into the bookstore. Jack Kendall was at the counter, scrutinizing what looked like an old book, which he hastily closed and shoved under that counter when she approached.

"I'm Samantha Halliwell from the Post," she said. "I was wondering if I could ask you a few questions about Rick Elliot."

Jack Kendall sighed and ran his hand through his graying hair. "I don't know what I can tell you," he said. "Rick just started working here."

"Did he ever mention anything about anyone that he had a problem with?" she asked. "Anyone who had some kind of gripe with him?"

Jack Kendall shook his head. "Not that I can remember." Behind her, the door opened and he looked over her shoulder to see who it was, before turning his attention back to her. "You'll have to excuse me, Ms. Halliwell."

Her brow furrowed. She still had more questions, but it wouldn't do any good to badger the man when he could still be a potential source. She could always come back to the bookstore. With that in mind, she smiled and thanked him for his time, then left the store, passing an elderly gentleman on her way out.

Once outside, she sat in her car for a few minutes, wondering who to talk to next. Rick Elliot's professors came to mind, but she quickly discounted them. They probably wouldn't know much more than Jack Kendall had. A girlfriend, perhaps? But she didn't know if Rick Elliot had even had one. That left a roommate. Again, she didn't know if he'd had one, but the university registrar would.

Getting the woman to give her the information was a little trickier than Samantha had thought it would be. She'd tried to smooth talk her, but the woman simply wouldn't budge. Samantha had been about to give up when the woman mentioned something about how much lunch cost in the college cafeteria. Surprisingly, all it took after that was a twenty-dollar bill for Samantha to walk out with a sticky note bearing Rick Elliot's address.

He had lived off campus in one of the apartment complexes nearby the university, instead of the dorms, and as luck would have it, he'd had a roommate. Fred Warden.

Fred was tall and what Samantha's grandmother would have called "pitifully skinny," with glasses that he constantly kept pushing up his nose. Whether out of nervousness or necessity, though, Samantha wasn't quite sure.

He looked at her curiously and she gave him a smile along with her customary introduction.

"I'm Samantha Halliwell from the Post," she said. "I was wondering if I could ask you a few questions about Rick Elliot."

He thought a moment before answering, then gave her a nod and stepped back so that she could enter. The living room was small and surprisingly tidy, if meagerly furnished with a mismatched and threadbare pair of sofas, a television that sat on a milk crate, and a small bookcase stuffed to the gills with well-worn paperback books. A beat-up looking coffee table was the only other furniture in the room.

Samantha took a seat on one of the sofas and reached into her shoulder bag for her notebook and pen. Fred Warden sat on the other sofa.

"Were you and Rick roommates for a while?" she asked.

He shook his head. "Since last semester." He looked down at the floor. "I couldn't believe it. I mean, I saw him before he went out last night. He was talking about this test he had today on impressionist artists." He shook his head again. "I can't believe it."

"Do you know of anyone who would do this to him?" she asked quietly.

Fred sighed. "He was one of those guys who got along with everybody, you know."

She nodded. "Did he ever talk about his job at the bookstore and whether he ever had a run-in with anyone there?"

"Not really," he said. "He liked working for Kendall, though. Said he was easygoing."

Samantha thought a moment. "Did Rick have a girlfriend?"

He shook his head. "He was seeing some girl at the beginning of the semester, I think, but they broke up." He gave her a sheepish look. "We didn't exactly hang out together, you know, so if he was going out with someone new, he didn't say." He paused. "Now that I think about it, though, from the way he talked, I'm pretty sure he was seeing someone. Not regularly, like a girlfriend or anything, more of a...well, you know."

She nodded that she did. "A booty call?"

He looked quickly down at the floor. "Yeah, I suppose so."

"And you don't know anything about her?"

"No, I don't know who she was," he said, still looking at the floor.

Samantha couldn't help but smile a little. This guy was so shy that he'd be lucky if he ever hooked up with anyone. She personally liked a guy who was confident. Though definitely not one who was arrogant like that detective, Hayden Tanner.

"Any idea where they hung out?" she asked Fred.

He thought a moment. "Not really. He was in and out at odd hours. But I know he liked to hang out at The Dorm Room, though. It's a bar and grill across from the university center."

She nodded and made some notes before looking at him. "Do you think I could take a look at his room?"

Fred Warden said nothing for a moment, indecision clearly written on his face. "I...I don't know," he said. "I mean, the cops haven't been here yet."

Samantha couldn't help feeling a bit superior upon learning that she had beaten the arrogant Detective Tanner to the punch. Score a point for her.

Across from her, Fred Warden still looked unsure and she hastened to reassure him.

"I promise that I won't disturb anything," she told him. "The cops won't even know I was here."

He thought about it some more, but then nodded and led her to Rick's room.

It was small and not nearly as neat as the living room. The bed was unmade, clothes had been tossed on the floor in a careless pile, and the closet door was half open. A poster of a swimsuit model hung on one wall and a corkboard complete with hastily scrawled notes written on odd-sized pieces of paper hung on the other. A pile of porno magazines was falling out of the bedside table.

It was the corkboard that caught Samantha's attention. Rick Elliot's handwriting left a lot to be desired, but she was able to decipher some of the notes. He was indeed supposed to have an exam on impressionist painters today, like Fred had said. There was also a reminder about his little sister's birthday. A note to call someone named Jen about studying for a French test. Nothing revealing or of any real help.

She glanced at the computer, her brow furrowing. Though Rick Elliot didn't look like he'd been a very organized person, computers were, by their nature, wonderful organizational tools.

The computer, however, didn't give her any more insight into Rick Elliot's life either. He had dozens of college papers, of course, which she didn't bother with. His schedule of classes did interest her, though, and she copied it down in her notebook. She had just begun reading through his email when the doorbell rang. She glanced at Fred, who excused himself to answer the door.

Rick Elliot had the usual junk mail from online stores he made purchases from as well as several emails from professors about assignments. There were also a handful from friends, mostly about this party or that party, but since Samantha didn't know what would be relevant and what wouldn't, she took notes on almost everything.

Finished, she put her notebook and pen back into her shoulder bag, neatened up the desk, or rather put it back the way she'd found it, and stood, only to turn and find herself face to face with Detective Tanner. He was leaning indolently against the doorframe, one shoulder propped against the wood, his arms folded across his chest, and he was glowering at her.

"Find anything interesting, Ms. Halliwell?" he asked.

His voice was soft, even, and very much like a caress, and despite herself, she shivered. Damn the man! "Nothing that would interest you, I'm sure." Inwardly, she groaned. So much for getting in good with the lead detective on the case.

"I could arrest you, you know," he said. "Let's see...there's tampering with evidence, for one thing. Oh, and let's not forget interfering with a police investigation, which is pretty much the same thing, though I'm sure it would carry a separate charge."

She lifted her chin. "I have permission to be in here and I can't tamper with evidence that doesn't exist. And I'm not interfering with a police investigation just because I got here before you did."

He lifted a brow and moved a step closer. "Then what do you call it?"

"Doing my job," she said.

"Really?" he countered. "Well, I'm pretty sure that a story on murder doesn't run in the arts and leisure section of the Post."

She felt color rise to her cheeks. "I'm getting into investigative reporting." She'd almost said that she was looking to move up, but then decided against it. No doubt, Detective Tanner would have something snide to say about that.

"Well, do it on some other story," he muttered, turning to go.

She frowned. "What's wrong with this story?" she demanded.

Her voice brought Hayden back around and he glared at her. Then swore under his breath.

When he didn't answer, she folded her arms and prompted him. "Well?"

"Because I don't want you under foot every time I turn around," he ground out.

Her lips curved. "Afraid I'm a better detective than you are?"

"I don't want you getting in my way!" he snapped.

She reached into her shoulder bag for her keys. "Then here's an idea," she said. "When you see me coming, pretend you don't, and I'll do the same."

Detective Tanner said nothing.

"Or you could simply work with me," she suggested. "Give me some information about the case."

He clenched his jaw. "Not a chance."

Samantha shrugged. "Then we'll go with Option A and ignore each other."

She started to push past him, but he caught her arm. Though his touch wasn't entirely ungentle, his hands were strong and powerful nonetheless.

"If you get in my way, I won't hesitate to arrest you, Ms. Halliwell," he warned her. Again, his voice was soft. Again, it made her shiver. "Is that understood?"

Samantha felt her pulse skip a beat at his authoritative tone of voice. It was clear that he was a man who expected to be obeyed. Perhaps it came with the territory. He was a cop, after all, used to being in charge. But it went deeper than that, she was sure. No doubt, he would be just as authoritative with a girlfriend or a wife. The idea made the butterflies in her stomach flutter with excitement.

Dammit, what was the matter with her? She'd gone to a strict private school as a child and had had enough of authority figures to last her a lifetime. She much preferred men who were polite and intellectual, men who treated her as a complete equal. Then why hadn't the relationships she'd had with men who'd been like that ever worked? a little voice in her head asked.

She lifted her chin. "You can't keep me from investigating this case with your threats, Detective, but by all means, you can continue to try if it makes you feel more of a man."

Hayden ground his jaw. He stood and watched her walk back into the living room, but didn't follow. Not until Samantha had thanked Fred Warden for his time and left the apartment.

Making his way into the living room, he looked at the college student. "Tell me everything you told her."

Chapter Two

Following the lead Fred Warden had given him, Hayden decided to stop by The Dorm Room that night. He was still pissed off that the kid had given Samantha Halliwell as much information as he had. Since she'd already made it clear that the threat of arrest wouldn't deter her from getting a story, Hayden was sure she'd show up at the bar and grill at some point – if she hadn't already – and start asking around about Rick Elliot.

The bar and grill was the preferred hangout among the university's students, so Hayden figured it would be a good place to ask questions. The Dorm Room's customers, however, weren't willing to talk to him or his badge. Disgusted he'd wasted his time, he weaved through the throng of people to the front door and pushed it open, nearly bumping into the woman who was coming in. He started to apologize, but the words froze on his lips when he recognized Samantha Halliwell.

She glared up at him for a moment, her eyes narrowing. Even in the soft light of the porch, he could see how blue they were. She took a step to the side, obviously set on ignoring him, and he stepped in front of her, blocking her path.

"Ms. Halliwell. Why am I not surprised to see you?" he drawled.

"I thought we agreed to ignore each other, Detective," she said stiffly.

They were blocking the main thoroughfare of the door, so Hayden took her arm and dragged her off to the side, ignoring the curious looks they were getting.

She tugged her arm free from his grasp and glared at him. "Is this a habit with you? Because if it is, it's really annoying."

He ignored her comment. "You agreed that we should ignore each other," he reminded her. "I told you that I'd arrest you."

She lifted a brow. "For having a drink and getting a bite to eat?"

He gave her a skeptical look. "At a college hangout?" Without her notebook and reading glasses, and her long, blonde hair down around her shoulders, he could almost forget she was a reporter.

She shrugged. "I heard they had good burgers."

He scowled. "Bull! You heard that Rick Elliot hung out here."

She gave him an innocent look. "Did he?"

He clenched his jaw. "You know damn well he did."

"Really?" She feigned surprise, her blue eyes going wide. "Do you think that someone might know something about the murder, then?"

Did she enjoy baiting him? he wondered. "You're pushing it, Ms. Halliwell."

She let out a sigh. "Look, I'm not going to interfere with your precious investigation and I'm not going to get in your way. I'm simply going to talk to a few of the regulars and see what they know about Rick Elliot."

He smirked, amused at the idea for some strange reason. "I already tried that and they weren't talking."

"Of course they wouldn't talk to you. I'm surprised your mother talks to you." She gave him a superior look. "But they will talk to me if they think I'm a fellow student."

Hayden said nothing for a moment. Damn, that could work. "Okay, but anything they tell you about Elliot, you tell me.

She smiled sweetly at him. "What are you going to do if I don't, Detective? Threaten to arrest me again? That really is starting to get old, you know."

His mouth quirked. He had a sudden vision of all the things he'd like to do to her, but the only thing he said was, "I'll put you

18

over my knee and spank that bottom of yours until you tell me what I want to know."

Hayden thought she'd be outraged by the idea, but from the way her eyes went a bit wide and her cheeks blushed, he'd say that Samantha Halliwell was as excited by the thought of being spanked as he was by the thought of spanking her.

"Do we have a deal, Ms. Halliwell?"

She wet her lips with the tip of her tongue and her voice was a little breathless when she spoke. "Yes, Detective. We have a deal."

As Hayden watched her walk up the steps, he found himself hoping Samantha Halliwell would call his bluff and withhold whatever information she learned.

Samantha wondered whether Hayden would make good on his promise if she refused to tell him what she discovered. The look in his eyes had told her that he would, and the thought gave her a sexy little thrill.

Though The Dorm Room was crowded, she managed to find a seat at the bar. Seeing that the bartender was busy at the other end, she took a moment to look around the room. Like a lot of other bars and restaurants in Seattle, the place had an eclectic style to it, with everything from sports equipment and pom-poms to yearbooks and a variety of other college memorabilia either hanging on the walls or dangling from the ceiling. The waitresses even sported the university's colors.

Maybe if she sat at the bar long enough, Samantha thought, Detective Tanner would get bored waiting for her and leave. She almost laughed; more likely, he'd grab her arm, drag her outside and put her over his knee. She blushed hotly at the thought.

"What can I get you?"

Banishing the arrogant detective from her mind, she looked at the bartender. He was young and cute, and she smiled at him. "Something tropical. Surprise me."

The bartender grinned and mixed her a colorful, fruity drink, which he placed on a cocktail napkin. "I don't think I've seen you before," he commented. "You new at the university?"

Samantha shook her head. "I just haven't ever been in here before. My friend came in sometimes with this guy she was seeing, though. Rick Elliot."

"Elliot?" He frowned. "The guy who was murdered?"

She nodded. "Did you know him?"

He shook his head. "No, not really. I mean, I've seen him a couple of times, but never talked to him or anything."

"I didn't know him that well, either." She sighed. "My friend says that he'd been acting weird, like he was keeping something from her. I think he was cheating on her, but she wouldn't believe it, and now... Well, now I suppose it doesn't matter, but I don't want her pining away for this guy if he was just a cheating jerk." She paused, as if thinking, and then took out her wallet. Inside was a picture of Samantha with her sister, which she showed to the bartender. "This is my friend. Have you seen him in here with anyone other than her?"

He looked at the picture for a moment, and then shook his head. "I never really saw him with any particular girl, not even this one. But he usually came in with a crowd, so I could have missed it."

Samantha nodded, putting her wallet back in her handbag. New customers crowded at the bar and he gave her nod. "Hope you find what you're looking for."

Samantha fingered the stem of her glass and glanced at the young man sitting beside her. He had a handsome profile, she thought, taking in the aquiline nose and strong chin.

As if sensing her scrutiny, he turned to her and grinned. "Rob," he introduced.

Samantha smiled. "Samantha."

"I heard you talking about Rick."

"Did you know him?" she asked.

He lifted his bottle of beer and took a long swallow before answering. "We had a few classes together."

"Really?" She looked at him with new interest.

20

"Yeah," he said. "I heard you talking about your friend."

She tried not to let her eagerness show. "Do you know if Rick was seeing someone, then?"

He downed the rest of the beer. "I don't know about that, but I do know what could have been making him act so weird."

"What's that?" she asked.

He glanced at the crowded tables. "We can't talk here."

Her brow furrowed. "Why?"

"Because the people involved wouldn't want me to be talking to anyone about it." His eyes held hers. "If you're really interested in hearing about it, let's go outside."

Samantha knew she should be wary of the invitation, but her desire to rub Detective Tanner's nose in the information she would get made her nod at the suggestion. Besides, the good detective was outside, so she'd be totally safe. Smiling, she stood and Rob put his arm around her waist to guide her around the tables. It was only after they'd made their way through the partying crowd that Samantha realized he was leading her to the back door of the bar.

Hayden glanced at his watch for what he was sure was the dozenth time and swore under his breath. What the hell was that woman doing? He wouldn't put it past her to deliberately keep him waiting. Then, in the same breath, he asked himself why he even cared. He was a cop with a job to do and she was a reporter he couldn't care less about. He should be out chasing down leads, not waiting for her outside some bar.

He'd talked to everybody in the place and hadn't gotten anything out of anybody because there was nothing to get. Then why was he standing outside like an idiot waiting for her?

He jerked the cuff of his jacket back and looked at his watch again. Damn. Maybe she'd gotten herself into trouble. Seeing as how she was so fond of sticking her nose in where it didn't belong, that wouldn't be a stretch to the imagination. Samantha Halliwell irritated the hell out of him, so it stood to reason she probably irritated the hell out of everyone. No doubt, she was in there harassing some poor college kids, making a nuisance of herself. He chastised himself. It was none of his business who she irritated. On second thought, if she found out something about Rick Elliot's murder, then it certainly was his business.

Telling himself that he was going inside merely to see if she'd learned anything useful, he walked up the steps and went inside.

The back door of the bar opened into the alley behind the building, and upon seeing that it was both dark and deserted, Samantha began to doubt her sanity. She didn't know anything about this guy, she told herself. Cute he may be, but he could also be some kind of weirdo. She folded her arms and looked at Rob, watching as he lit a cigarette and then took a deep drag on it.

"So, what kind of information do you have?" she asked, glancing around the darkened alley nervously.

Rob leaned back against the wall and boldly looked her up and down. "What's it worth to you?"

Samantha looked up at him with wide eyes. Was he talking about money? What was it with these people? First the registrar, and now this guy. Did she have "expense account" stamped on her forehead? "What do you mean? I'm just trying to help out my friend."

"Are you a cop?" he asked, accusation in his eyes.

She took a step back, laughing nervously. What would make him think that? "Of course not."

"Then why the questions?" he demanded. "What are you, some wacko, murder, cult freak or something?"

Samantha didn't think you could use all those adjectives in one sentence. She shivered and told herself that it was the night air. "I told you, I'm just trying to help out my friend. She's taking this really hard." She forced herself to relax. "So, if you have any dirt on Rick, it'd really help."

Rob inhaled deeply on the cigarette. "Am I gonna get any money outta this?"

"I...uh...I don't really have much."

He studied her for a moment. "What do you want to know about Elliot?"

"Anything you can tell me. You know, the stuff he wouldn't want a girlfriend to know."

"Rick owed people money, I can tell you that. He was always looking to borrow."

"That's not so odd for a college student," she pointed out.

He snorted. "I'm not talking a few bucks. I'm talking about thousands."

She frowned. "He had expensive tastes, then. Or an expensive habit."

Rob's cigarette glowed orange in the darkened alley. "I heard that he owed the wrong people some money."

"Do you know who?" Samantha prompted.

He stared at her for a few moments, the look suspicious. "For someone who's not a cop, you sure ask questions like a cop."

"I told you, I'm not a cop," she said sharply. "Do you have any idea who he owed?"

Rob tossed the cigarette on the floor of the alley. "No. So, how about that payment you promised?"

She frowned. "Look, I'm not made out of money. I can give you a few dollars, I suppose."

He looked her up and down, then took a step closer. She tried to sidestep him, but he grabbed her arm. Her gasp of outrage came out as an "oomph!" as he pushed her roughly against the wall.

"That's okay. I'm sure we can work something else out," he said, his face close to hers.

He'd trapped her between the wall and his body, and Samantha looked up at him wide-eyed. His breath was hot on her face and he smelled of beer and cigarettes. She'd been crazy to come outside with him. Oh yeah, this had been a really, really stupid idea. She could be raped out here in this dark alley. This guy could kill her.

"Look, I'm just a reporter," she said, her voice trembling. "I don't have much on me now, but I can try to get more."

He smirked, his gaze slithering over her. "I didn't say it had to be money," he said, his fingers brushing the side of her face.

She jerked back from his touch. "Look, my boyfriend's a cop," she said, the lie rolling easily off her tongue. Where had that come from? she wondered frantically as she tried to push against him.

He laughed. "What, does he have you doing his dirty work for him?"

His hands tightened on her shoulders and Samantha felt the rough cut of the wall dig painfully into her back as he pressed her against it. Taking a breath, she started to scream, but he clamped his hand tightly over her mouth, effectively muffling the noise. Samantha found some unfamiliar, detached part of herself wondering if Detective Tanner would come looking for her. Not likely. No, she'd gotten herself into this; she'd have to get herself out.

She was frantically trying to think of some way to do that when a loud noise startled both her and Rob. He loosened his grip on her mouth and she pulled free to let out a loud scream.

Rob swore and immediately released her to race out of the alley. Samantha leaned back against the wall and closed her eyes, grateful for the interruption. Footsteps raced down the alley in her direction, then came to a stop in front of her. She lifted her gaze to find Detective Tanner standing before her.

Hayden stared at the opening of the alley before turning his attention to her. Shoving his gun into its holster, he reached out and gently put his hands on her shoulders. "Are you okay?"

Samantha nodded. She was still trembling and the warmth of his hands through the thin material of her shirt felt good. "Yes."

Hayden regarded her for a moment in silence, and then swore under his breath. "What the hell were you doing out here?"

She lifted her head to look at him. "I was getting information."

"Really? Well, that was a stupid way to go about it."

She flushed. "I didn't know he was going to try something," she snapped, flinging off his hands with her own. "He was telling me about Rick Elliot, and then he started talking about getting paid for the information. I told him that I didn't have much on me and he..." her voice trailed off and she saw Hayden's mouth tighten.

"What did he tell you?"

She shrugged. "Just that Rick owed the wrong people money."

He nodded. "Did he give you a name?"

She shook her head. "But considering what he wanted from me, I'm wondering if he was even telling the truth."

Hayden said nothing for a moment, and then glanced at the mouth of the alley again. "Come on, I'll take you home."

"I have my car."

"I'll follow you, then."

Her brow furrowed. "That's not necessary. I'm fine."

"I said, I'd follow you," he said curtly.

She sighed, knowing it would be easier to give in than to argue with him. "Fine."

Hayden's eyes narrowed at her tone, but he said nothing, and they made their way to their respective cars in silence.

Once at her apartment, Samantha thought Hayden would consider his good deed done and leave, but he surprised her by walking her to her door. Unlocking it, she pushed it open before turning back to him.

"Thank you, Detective," she said. "I think I can take it from here."

His mouth tightened. "We're not finished."

She lifted a brow. "I can't think of what else we have to discuss."

"I can," was all he said.

She sighed in exasperation. "Fine. Come in, then."

Walking into the living room, she tossed her purse on the couch before making her way into the adjoining kitchen. Hayden followed.

"I won't bother to offer you anything since you won't be staying," she said as she opened the fridge and took out a bottle of water.

"What you did at that bar was beyond stupid, Samantha." Hayden's mouth tightened. "If I hadn't come looking for you..."

"I would have managed," she told him hotly.

He lifted a brow. "Really? Just what would you have done?"

That caught her off guard. "I...I don't know. But I would have thought of something." She set the bottle of water down on the counter. "Now, if you don't mind..."

She started past him, but Hayden caught her arm. "I'm not finished."

Before Samantha knew what he was doing, Hayden was seated on one of the kitchen chairs with her over his knee.

For a moment, she was too stunned to do more than just lay there, then abruptly realizing what he intended, she struggled. To keep her still, he clamped one arm over her waist, holding her firmly in place while he rested his free hand on her upturned bottom. Even through the material of her skirt, she could feel the heat from his skin.

"What are you doing?" she demanded, craning her neck to see over her shoulder.

"Making sure that you don't pull a stunt like that again."

"But you can't...*oh!*" she let out a gasp of surprise as her smacked her bottom. She couldn't believe it – he was actually spanking her!

"Oh, but I can," he said.

His hand came down again, harder this time, and she let out another cry.

"My job is to serve and protect," he continued, spanking her again. "It just so happens that in this case, it means protecting you from yourself."

He spanked her again, hard enough to sting, and she cried out. "Okay, you've made your point."

Hayden laughed softly. "I'm just getting warmed up, Samantha."

Just getting warmed up? Her brow furrowed. What did he mean by that?"

But she soon found out as he ran his hand up her leg to slowly lift her skirt, exposing her panty-clad bottom.

Samantha blushed. "Detective..."

"Hayden," he said.

"Hayden..." She caught her breath as his hand cupped her bottom. The thin bikini panties she wore would offer little protection from a spanking, and though she knew she should protest, she didn't. Instead, she was tingling with the anticipation of having a man as handsome and sexy as Hayden Tanner give her a spanking. She should be furious with him, she told herself. The man was a brute!

Abruptly, he lifted his hand and brought it down hard on her right cheek.

"*Owww!*"

The next spank came down on her left cheek, a little harder. After that, he fell into an easy rhythm, alternating from one cheek to the other amid "*Oh's!* and "*Ow's!*", all the while holding her firmly as she struggled and wiggled.

"Just a few more," Hayden said.

"But it hurts," she protested.

"It's supposed to hurt," he told her. "That's why it's called a spanking."

"Please..." she pleaded. It really was beginning to hurt, and by now she was sure that her bottom was as red as her face had been moments before. "I've learned my lesson," she told him. "Really."

"Really?" He sounded amused.

"Yes," she said quickly. "No more sneaking into dark alleys with strange men. I promise."

"Good. Because if I have to put you over my knee again for doing something so foolish, the next spanking will be on your bare bottom," Hayden said.

His words brought an image so vivid and erotic to mind that Samantha could no longer ignore the tingling between her thighs, or how aroused she was becoming. But before she could do more than contemplate what that meant, Hayden was spanking her again. Not hard enough to hurt her, but hard enough that she wouldn't soon forget being over his knee, and it was only after he was satisfied she'd been sufficiently punished that he let her up.

But he didn't let her go. They stood looking at each other in silence for a moment. Hayden's gaze was so intense that Samantha blushed and almost looked away. But as if he'd somehow guessed that she was thinking, he gently lifted her chin with a forefinger.

"No more detective work, Samantha."

Her brow furrowing, she opened her mouth to argue and his face darkened.

"I mean it, Samantha," he said softly. "Unless you want another spanking."

The words sent a delicious shiver of anticipation down her back, but her bottom was still too warm for her to entertain the thought of another spanking at the moment. That, and she wanted to get his mind on something else – like kissing her! So, she nodded and told him what he wanted to hear.

"No more detective work."

"Good."

Hayden stood looking down at her for another long moment, and Samantha waited expectantly, her lips parted in invitation. But before either of them could make a move, the door to her apartment opened and her roommate sailed in.

"You wouldn't believe the day I had..." Alexa began as she came into the kitchen, but then stopped abruptly when she saw Hayden. "Oh!"

Hayden dropped his hand and took a step back. Samantha silently grumbled about her pretty, dark-haired roommate's timing, while at the same time wondering how she could have forgotten the girl. Alexa could have walked in while Hayden was spanking her!

"Hayden, this is my roommate, Alexa," she said quietly. "Alexa – Hayden Tanner."

They exchanged pleasantries, after which Alexa very intuitively excused herself, leaving Samantha alone with Hayden.

Neither of them spoke for a moment, and then Hayden gently tucked a strand of hair behind her ear. "If I come by the Post tomorrow night, would you have dinner with me?" he said softly.

Samantha's pulse quickened. "I'd like that," she said breathlessly.

"Good." At the door, he turned and eyed her warningly. "Remember, Samantha – no more detective work."

When she said nothing, he lifted a brow and she was reluctantly forced to agree, even though she had no intention of keeping her promise. What Hayden didn't know, wouldn't hurt him, she told herself. And provided that she didn't get herself into trouble, there was no reason Hayden would find out what she was up to.

If he did find out, though... Well, he would almost assuredly spank her again, she thought, and the image of the handsome detective putting her over his knee for another spanking made her pulse race with delicious anticipation.

Chapter Three

Despite her promise to Hayden – and his threat of another spanking – Samantha spent the next day investigating. After making an appearance at the paper and having a quick meeting with her editor, she headed back over to the university to talk to some of Rick Elliot's classmates.

But no one seemed to know anything about the woman Rick Elliot had supposedly been seeing, which made Samantha wonder why he'd been so secretive about her. Was she married? That could definitely be worth checking into.

No one knew anything about him owing anyone any money, either, except for a few bucks here and there. Which probably meant that jerk from the bar had been lying, she thought bitterly.

But since they were the only leads she had, they were worth further investigation, which brought her back to the bookstore where he had worked.

The store's owner, Jack Kendall, was nowhere to be found, however. In fact, the store seemed to be empty.

"Mr. Kendall," she called.

The store was small and charming, full of books and cozy alcoves that had inviting window seats and comfortable chairs to curl up in. Though Samantha preferred the chain stores that offered a bigger selection of books and well-stocked coffee bars, there was something to be said for the quaint, little bookstore, she thought as she wandered around.

"Mr. Kendall," she called again, a little louder this time.

Still no answer.

Figuring he must just be in the back room, she decided to wait for the older man, and walked up to the front of the store. There was a large stack of paperback books on the counter, which wouldn't have been worth noting if not for the fact that the covers had been ripped off. But right beside the stack of books was a pile of book covers that looked like they had just come from a printer. She picked one up. Strange. She had never thought about it, but apparently, small bookstores had to glue their own covers on.

"Can I help you?"

Samantha jumped at the sound of Jack Kendall's voice and whirled around to face him, the book cover still in her hand. His eyes immediately locked on it and she put it back on the counter, feeling strangely guilty at having been caught looking at it.

"Mr. Kendall," she said, giving him a smile. "I've been waiting to talk to you."

He walked around the counter and collected the book covers up before looking at her, and when he did, his gaze was wary. "Oh?"

"About Rick Elliot."

He took the covers and stuffed them beneath the counter, his hands trembling slightly. He knew something about Rick Elliot's murder, she thought.

"I don't know what else I can tell you about him," he said, avoiding her gaze.

"I spoke with a guy who said that Rick owed people some money, and I was wondering if he ever mentioned needing extra cash," she said.

He frowned and adjusted his eyeglasses. "Not that I remember. Rick was very responsible, which was the reason I hired him. He came in on time, did his work, and locked up the store when I needed him to."

Her brow furrowed. "I thought you said he'd only been working for you a short time."

Kendall picked up a stack of books and came around the counter. "He did, but in that time, he proved himself to be very competent," the older man said, walking away from her.

Undeterred, Samantha followed. "Did he ever ask you to give him an advance on his pay?" she asked.

Kendall placed one of the books on the shelf. "No, he didn't."

"Did he ever ask you to lend him money?" she persisted.

He walked down the row and placed another book on another shelf. "No, he did not."

She nodded. "Did any of his friends ever stop by while he was working?"

He shrugged. "I suppose."

"Do you remember if any of those friends were women?" she asked. "Any that you remember seeing repeatedly? Like a girlfriend, perhaps?"

"I really couldn't say." He gave her an impatient look. "I'm very busy, Ms. Halliwell."

She frowned. What was the man hiding? It was like he couldn't seem to get rid of her fast enough.

"Of course." Taking out her spiral notebook and a pen, she wrote her cell phone number on one of the pages, then tore it off and held it out to him. "If you do think of anything, though, would you call me?" she said.

He hesitated for a moment before giving her a curt nod. "Of course," he said, taking the number.

She smiled, thanked him for his time, and then left the bookstore. She wanted to chalk the day up as a waste of time, but then chided herself for being so negative. Just because no one knew if Elliot owed anyone money, that didn't mean he hadn't. Nor did it mean that Elliot hadn't been seeing some mystery woman, Samantha told herself. She just had to dig deeper.

Of course, that would mean getting in good with the lead detective on the case, and she didn't think Hayden would be any more receptive to the idea of them working together now than he'd been before, regardless of the fact that he'd asked her to have dinner with him. He seemed to have this crazy notion that she was going to get herself into trouble, which was ridiculous. Admittedly, going out into a dark alley with a stranger had been irresponsible on her part, but she wouldn't do something that stupid again. She truly had learned her lesson when it came to that. Perhaps she would mention how odd Kendall had been acting and let Hayden check into the guy's background. Surely, that would show him how responsible she was being.

Hayden looked up as his partner sat down at the desk opposite his. Nik had gone to pick up the forensic report and from the look on his face, it was obvious that the findings weren't going to be much help in solving Rick Elliot's murder.

"Nothing, and I mean nothing," Nik said. "The ME said it looked like whoever murdered Elliot washed him clean before they dumped the body, because there's no evidence. No blood, no semen, nothing. Other than a few beers, Elliot's tox screen came back clean, too." Nik sighed and gestured to the paper in front of Hayden. "How about you?"

Hayden glanced at the list of numbers. He'd been checking Elliot's phone records for anything out of the ordinary, but had come up empty. He shook his head. "I got nothing, either."

Nik sat back in his chair and shook his head. "So, we've got no motive, no murder weapon, and no crime scene. Hell, we can't even find anyone who disliked the guy."

That was true enough, Hayden thought. No one had a bad word to say about Rick Elliot, and without a motive to work with, they couldn't even begin to come up with a list of suspects. Though his gut told him the guy who had cornered Samantha outside The Dorm Room the night before had been lying about Elliot owing someone money, Hayden and Nik had checked into it anyway. But again, they'd come up empty. None of the bookmakers in town knew anything about Elliot having a gambling habit.

As he and his partner sat in silence, contemplating their next move, their boss, Captain Conner, came by to check their progress on the case.

"So, what do we got?" he asked.

A soft-spoken, unassuming man, Martin Conner wasn't the type to constantly peer over his detectives' shoulders, which, in Hayden's opinion, made him ideal to work for.

"Forensics didn't come up with anything," Nik said.

"Elliot's phone records were a bust, too," Hayden added.

Conner nodded. "Well, I have the chief breathing down my neck. Dead students on campus don't look good for the university."

"Elliot's roommate said that he was seeing some girl, but he didn't know who she was," Hayden told him. "We're still looking into it."

The older man shrugged. "Get a list of every girl in every class Elliot had, and go through the names." He gave them a pointed look. "If she's out there, I want her found."

Nik looked at Hayden. "I guess it's back to the university tomorrow, then," he said after Conner had left. He glanced at his watch. "Hey, do you want to come over for dinner? Krista's making this new recipe. Some kind of Mexican lasagna, I think."

Hayden stood. Nik's wife was a terrific cook and if he didn't have a date with Samantha, then he would have accepted the invitation without hesitation. But he did have a date with Samantha...something he didn't want his partner to know. Nik would rib him enough as it was when he found out. If things with Samantha even went that far, he thought.

Hayden still couldn't believe that he'd suggested they have dinner together. She was a reporter, which, for obvious reasons, meant that a relationship with her could never work.

Or could it? He was older, wiser, and a hell of a lot more experienced than he'd been when he'd dated Jessica, that was for sure. He knew better than to allow himself to be played for a fool again. He'd simply keep his personal life separate from his work.

"Hayden?"

He looked at Nik. His partner had stood and was regarding him curiously. "Um...actually, I gotta pass," Hayden said, getting to his feet. "I have some things to do."

Nik's brow furrowed. "With the case?"

Hayden shook his head, but didn't look at his partner as they left the station house.

As her date with Hayden drew closer, the more Samantha found herself looking forward to seeing the handsome detective again. Regardless of the hostility between them when they'd first met, she couldn't ignore the fact that she'd been incredibly attracted to him even then. But after he'd put her over his knee and spanked her – she still couldn't think about it without blushing – Samantha had no doubt that she and Hayden would have ended up in bed if her roommate hadn't come in. Which, for her, would have been very uncharacteristic.

It wasn't that she was a prude or anything. It was simply that she liked to get to know a guy before she slept with him. Admittedly, she hadn't had that many relationships, but none of the men she'd ever dated had made her want to jump into bed with them as quickly as Hayden had. Then again, none of those other men had ever spanked her, either.

Pulling into the Post's parking garage, she quickly found a space, which wasn't too difficult since most everyone had already left for the day. Grabbing her shoulder bag from the seat beside her, she stepped out of the car and started to make her way toward the building.

Suddenly, out of nowhere, a car came speeding down the aisle. Samantha stood rooted to the floor for a moment, staring at the car careening toward her with wide eyes.

Finally able to force herself to move, she jumped backward out of the way just as the car sped by. She fell awkwardly on her side between two parked cars. If they hadn't been there to shield her, she almost certainly would have been run over. The other car hadn't even slowed down either. There was a squeal of tires and a crunching sound before it disappeared out of sight around a corner. She heard the screeching of tires for several more moments before that, too, disappeared.

"Ms. Halliwell!" a man's voice called out. "Are you okay?"

Samantha looked up to see the Post's evening security guard hurrying toward her. Short and slightly overweight, he was out of breath and muttering something about crazy drivers as he reached her side.

She pushed herself up into a sitting position, intending to get to her feet, but the security guard put his hand on her shoulder.

"Take it easy, Ms. Halliwell," he advised. "You took quite a tumble."

Heedless of his advice, she proceeded to get to her feet and winced at the pain that lanced through her shoulder. Cupping her shoulder with her other hand, she squeezed gently, testing the area to see how badly she'd been hurt. She was sore and the palms of her hands felt raw from where they had scraped the concrete, but other than that, everything seemed intact.

"I'll get you some help," the security guard said. He was looking at her oddly, as if he expected her to pass out at any moment.

She shook her head, still massaging her shoulder. "That's not necessary, John. I'm fine."

He didn't look convinced. "I don't know, Ms. Halliwell..."

"Samantha?"

Samantha looked up at the familiar voice to see Hayden coming toward them. His brow was furrowed and he was looking at her in concern.

"What happened?" he asked.

She gave him a small smile, trying to shrug it off. "Nothing..."

"Some guy almost ran her down!" the security guard told him.

Hayden looked at her in disbelief. "What?!"

"It was nothing, really," she said quickly. "It was probably just someone not paying attention to how fast he was going. I'm fine."

"I still think I should call the cops," the security guard said.

Hayden shot the man a quick look. "I am a cop." He looked at Samantha. "What happened?"

37

She shook her head. "I don't know. He didn't see me or I wasn't paying attention, I guess."

The security guard snorted. "I wouldn't say that he didn't see her," he huffed. "The minute she stepped into the thruway, he sped up. It was like he was trying to deliberately run her down."

Samantha frowned. It had happened so fast that she really couldn't remember it very clearly at all.

"Did you get a plate number?" Hayden asked the security guard.

The man gave him a sheepish look. "No, but it was a sedan. Dark red, I think." He paused. "After he nearly ran Ms. Halliwell down, he almost took out that concrete support on his way out."

Hayden and Samantha followed the security guard's gaze to see a smear of dark colored paint on the concrete.

The security guard looked from Hayden to Samantha. "Well, if you're not going to file any paperwork, I guess I'll get back to work." He hesitated. "If you're sure you're okay, I mean," he said to Samantha.

She gave him a small smile. "I really am," she said, and then glanced at Hayden.

"Okay, then..." he gave Hayden a nod before moving off.

Hayden reached out and tucked a strand of hair behind her ear. "You really should see a doctor, you know," he said quietly.

She dismissed the notion with a shake of her head. "I'm fine." He still looked unconvinced. "Hayden, really," she added with a smile.

He regarded her for a moment and she thought he would insist, but he didn't. "Look, if you'd like to do dinner another time..."

She sighed. "Hayden, I'm fine. The car didn't even touch me, and contrary to what the security guard thinks, I'm sure it wasn't deliberate."

Hayden shrugged. "It could have been."

She looked at him incredulously. "Who would want to hurt me?"

"The guy who tried to attack you at the bar last night," he said without hesitation.

She frowned. "You think he'd try to kill me over what happened in that alley?"

Hayden shrugged. "If he was pissed off enough, maybe." He thought a moment. "Or if he murdered Elliot and thinks you're onto him."

"You think he murdered Elliot?" she asked eagerly.

His expression hardened. "I didn't spank you hard enough last night, did I, Samantha?"

She blushed. "I...I was just asking."

He continued to glower at her. "You were hoping I'd give you a scoop and I won't."

She folded her arms and glared right back at him. "You know, if you'd cooperate with me, I wouldn't have to sneak around behind your back to get my story."

His jaw tightened. "I won't discuss the case with you, Samantha, and if that's the only reason you agreed to have dinner with me, then you're wasting your time."

"Of course it wasn't!" she protested. "I agreed because I..."

When she hesitated, he lifted a brow. "You what?"

She felt herself blushing again. What could she say? That she agreed to have dinner with him because she'd been incredibly turned on by the spanking he'd given her? "I agreed because despite your Neanderthal ways, I find that I'm attracted to you."

He grinned. "Or maybe you're attracted to me because you like my Neanderthal ways."

She blushed even deeper. "Are we going to dinner, or what?"

He laughed and led the way to his Wrangler, which was parked nearby.

"I thought we'd have dinner at my place, if that's okay with you?" he said as they drove.

That was more than okay with her, she thought, eager to be alone with him. "Are you a good cook, then?"

His mouth quirked. "I've been known to make a pretty good pasta on occasion."

Actually, Hayden made a very good pasta, she thought as they had dinner a little while later. Though Samantha wasn't known for her skills in the kitchen, she had offered to make the salad, and once that was done, she'd perched on the counter and then watched in fascination as he'd added a touch of cream and some sugar to the homemade sauce.

"I don't think I've ever seen anyone actually make homemade sauce before. I feel like I'm watching the cooking channel," she'd said with a laugh.

He'd let out a soft, sexy chuckle. "We Neanderthals can do more than hunt woolly mammoth, you know."

Samantha had just laughed.

Conversation came just as easy during dinner, too, probably because they didn't talk about the case, she thought wryly. But they did talk about everything else, including their families, where they grew up, their likes and dislikes, even their interests, many of which they shared, something that came as a pleasant surprise to Samantha. She'd been half afraid that despite their attraction to each other, she and Hayden would have nothing else in common.

After dinner, however, Samantha couldn't contain her curiosity any more and turned the conversation back to the investigation.

"So, did you ever track down the guy Rick Elliot owed money to?" she asked as they were cleaning up the kitchen.

Hayden slanted her a hard look, but said nothing as he continued to dry the pasta pot.

"Hayden, come on," she cajoled. "I should at least know what happened with the lead, especially since I was the one who gave it to you."

He leaned back against the counter and folded his arms with a sigh. "If I tell you, will you stop digging?"

She said nothing.

"Samantha..." he warned.

She sighed. "Okay," she snapped.

Hayden frowned. "I asked around. Elliot owed a few bucks here and there, but that was all."

She nodded. "I asked around, too, and that's what they told me as well."

"You went back to the university to ask questions after what happened last night?" he asked incredulously.

"It's not like I was talking to some creep in a dark alley again, Hayden," she protested.

His jaw tightened. "I told you what would happen if I learned that you'd been playing detective again."

Samantha felt herself blush. "I wasn't playing detective, I was doing my job," she objected.

His frowned deepened and he regarded her with a stern expression. "Regardless, I thought I made it painfully clear that I didn't want you snooping, Samantha, but I see that you need a reminder."

"Hayden, I don't..." she started to protest, but as he took her hand and led across the kitchen to a chair, her traitorous pulse began to race in anticipation and she forgot whatever it was she was about to say.

This time Hayden didn't even give her a warm up over her skirt, but simply pushed aside the flowing material once she was over his knee and started in on her panty-clad bottom. Samantha blushed as she imagined him gazing down at her bikini panties. They were so skimpy that they were barely enough to cover her bottom, and she could only hope they provided some protection. Not that it mattered, though, because after a dozen or so sharp spanks, he had the thin scrap of silk down around her thighs.

Samantha's color deepened. She held her breath, waiting for Hayden to continue with her spanking, but instead he gently caressed her already hot and stinging bottom. She moaned softly, part of her wanting him to forget all about spanking her so they could hurry up and make love, while the other part wanted him to redden her bottom until she was so aroused that she couldn't think straight.

Abruptly, Hayden lifted his hand and brought it down hard, eliciting a soft cry of protest, which only earned her another spank, followed by another and another, each one harder than the one before it.

"*Oh!*" she gasped. How could something that stung so fiercely feel so unbelievably good? she wondered as his hand continued to fall over and over on her bare ass.

But in spite of how good it felt to have her bottom warmed, Samantha couldn't help but squirm. That didn't deter Hayden in the least. He merely tightened his hold around her waist and administered smack after stinging smack.

By the time he had finished, Samantha's ass felt like it was glowing, and when he finally let her up, she couldn't resist the urge to press her hands to her stinging cheeks. Her skin was unbelievably hot and sensitive to the touch, both of which only seemed to heighten her arousal, and she almost asked where the bathroom was just so she could look in the mirror to see how red it was.

But then Hayden bent his head to kiss her and all thought fled her mind. His mouth was hot on hers, his tongue demanding as it swept into her mouth to tangle with hers. Samantha melted against him with a moan, her hands gliding up the front of his shirt to grasp his shoulders. With a groan, he dragged his mouth away from hers to trail kisses along her jaw and down her neck. Her knees went weak and she clung to him, afraid that if she didn't, she would melt into a puddle of goo right there on the floor.

"Samantha, I want you," he said hoarsely.

"Yes…" she breathed.

He ran his hands down her arms to her slim waist, then under the hem of her shirt and up to her breasts where he gently rubbed the pads of his thumbs over her nipples. They hardened under the thin material of her bra and she let out a husky moan.

He kissed her lips again, his mouth slowly moving over hers, his hands gliding under her skirt to cup her well-spanked bottom. His touch was firm on her tender skin, and she sighed with pleasure.

From somewhere, a ringing phone sounded. Samantha ignored it, hoping that if she did, it would stop. But to her dismay, it didn't.

Swearing softly, Hayden lifted his head and drew in a ragged breath as he pulled his cell phone from his pocket.

"Yeah," he said, and then listened for a moment. "Okay, I'll be right there."

Samantha watched as Hayden flipped the phone closed and shoved in back into his pocket. He looked so gorgeous standing there that all she wanted was for him to pick her up and take her to bed, but she knew from the expression on his face that the call he'd gotten had been important. And that it was also going to interrupt what they had just started.

He reached out to tuck a strand of hair behind her ear. "I have to go out for a bit," he said, tracing her lips with his thumb. "Wait for me?"

Samantha nodded.

Hayden gazed down at her hungrily for a long moment in silence. With a groan, he bent his head and covered her mouth with his in a searing kiss that left her breathless. Not to mention wanting more.

"I'll be back as quick as I can," he said.

Despite how turned on she was, Samantha couldn't contain her curiosity as she watched him strap on his shoulder holster. "Do you have a lead on Rick Elliot?"

His eyes narrowed warningly. "Samantha..."

"Okay, forget I asked," she muttered.

He shrugged into his jacket, then studied her thoughtfully for a moment before pulling her close for another kiss.

Samantha stood staring at the door. Her first inclination was to follow Hayden, but then she thought of the spanking he'd just given her and decided against it. Her bottom was still stinging.

Going over to the fridge, she poured a glass of milk, then grabbed a paperback book from the well-read collection that Hayden had before settling herself on the couch. The book she'd chosen was a crime-thriller. Though it wasn't something she'd normally read, it was all the handsome detective had.

She was just getting into the story when her phone rang. Grabbing her shoulder bag, she took out her cell phone and held it to her ear.

"Hello."

"Ms. Halliwell?" asked a man's voice.

"Yes."

"It's Jack Kendall. From the bookstore." A pause. "I wanted to apologize for being so curt with you today. I was just very busy."

Her brow burrowed. "Of course," she said, wondering what the man wanted.

"But I did remember some information about Rick that could be helpful, if you're interested," he continued.

Her pulse quickened. "Yes, I am."

He paused again. "I'd prefer to talk in person. Can you come by the store?"

She glanced at her watch and frowned. It was almost ten o'clock. "Now?"

"Yes. I know it's late, but this is a difficult subject to talk about over the phone. The repercussions could be felt by more people than just Rick. I hope you understand."

Samantha hesitated. Hayden would be furious with her for going off to investigate, especially after he'd repeatedly warned her against it. But it sounded as if the owner of the bookstore had something really juicy. It could make the story.

"I'll be there in twenty minutes," she told Jack Kendall.

Chapter Four

Jack Kendall was waiting by the door for her when she got to the bookstore. Unlocking the door, he let her inside, and then locked it again, muttering something about it being after closing time. The store was dark, lit only by a small lamp in the back, but in the light from the outside streetlamp, she could see that his hands were trembling.

"No one came with you, did they?" he asked, nervously glancing out the window.

She shook her head, her brow furrowing in confusion. "No."

Kendall nodded. "Good." He paused. "Let's talk in the back, shall we?"

He held out his hand, indicating that she should walk ahead of him, which she did, making her way through the dimly lit store to the small reading table on which the lamp sat.

"So," she said, turning to face him. "On the phone, you mentioned you had something to tell me about Rick Elliot?"

Kendall stood looking at her for a moment, an odd expression on his face. "Actually, I'm more interested in what you know, Ms. Halliwell."

"What I know?" She frowned. "About Rick Elliot?"

"About me."

She looked at him in confusion. "I don't think I understand."

"Don't play games with me, Ms. Halliwell," he said sharply. "We both know what you saw, and we both know that you're not going to keep quiet about it."

She thought a moment, trying to think what he was referring to. What had she seen? "Mr. Kendall, I don't know what you're talking about."

"Do you know what it's like to run a bookstore, Ms. Halliwell?" he asked abruptly. "People don't come in here to buy books. They come in here to sit in the comfortable chairs I have and read them while they're waiting for the movie down the street to start." He let out a short, harsh laugh. "Then you know what they do? They put the books back on the shelves – usually the wrong shelves – and walk out."

Samantha wasn't sure why he was telling her this or where the conversation was going, but she really wanted to get back to Hayden's apartment before he found that she'd gone out. "Mr. Kendall..." she began.

"It takes a lot to run a bookstore," he continued as if she hadn't spoken. "I have to pay for rent, utilities, and advertising, not to mention the shopping bags I have to buy or the employees I have to hire. Then, on top of all that, I still have to have money set aside to purchase books."

Samantha tried again. "Mr. Kendall, what is this about?"

"You know perfectly well what this is about. It's about the stripped books."

She shook her head, still confused. "What are stripped books?"

"Don't act like you don't know. You've already seen them. The stack of books on the counter that had their covers torn off," he told her. "You know what I've been doing and that's what your real story is about."

"Um..." She frowned. "I'm really only interested in your employee, Rick. I don't have anything to do with writing about the publishing world."

But Kendall didn't seem to even have heard her. His eyes had a slightly glazed look to them and his brow was wrinkled in a frown. "I take the covers off and send them back to the publisher, who in turn gives me a credit for those books with the understanding that I will destroy them." He paused, adjusting his glasses. "I used to do that, get rid of the books like I was supposed to, I mean. But then I thought of the money I could make if I simply put new covers on the books and sold them anyway."

Samantha thought back to the stack of books and the covers she'd seen on the counter that afternoon, and realization slowly began to dawn on her. "Which would be illegal," she said quietly.

"Only if someone found out," he said. "I didn't think anyone would find out."

His voice had taken on an odd note and she took a step back, suddenly uneasy. "But Rick Elliot did find out, and so you murdered him."

Jack Kendall looked at her in surprise. "Rick? I didn't murder Rick." He shook his head. "I was talking about you finding out."

Her mouth went dry and she took another step back. The back of her legs came up against the arm of the chair that was behind her and she hastily stepped around it. Chasing down a lead with the harmless bookstore owner had suddenly become as dangerous as ducking into that back alley had been.

"I can't let you leave, Ms. Halliwell, not knowing what you know," he said. "I could lose the store, probably even go to jail. I could certainly never pay all the fines and legal fees."

As he spoke, Jack Kendall reached for the heavy bookend that was on the table and took a step toward her.

Hayden was surprised to find Samantha gone when he got back to the apartment. At first, he thought she'd just gotten tired of waiting and gone back to her place, but then he found the hastily written note she'd left on the kitchen table.

Hayden,
I went to see Jack Kendall about a
lead. It's perfectly safe, so don't be mad.
Please.
Samantha

Mad! Hayden clenched his jaw, his hand tightening on the paper. He was furious with her! What the hell was she thinking, going off to chase down a lead, especially after what had happened in that alley last night? When he got his hands on her...

He shook his head. He'd been too easy on her before, he realized. He'd thought that another spanking would deter her from any more foolishness, but apparently, Samantha needed an additional lesson, and this time, he vowed, she wouldn't soon forget it.

Swearing under his breath, Hayden grabbed his keys from where he'd tossed them on the counter and left the apartment.

In all honesty, he had half expected Samantha to follow him to the university. He had even found himself looking for her in the crowd of people that had gathered around the dining hall, which was where the most recent victim had been found.

The MO was the same as Elliot's murder. The victim, a white male, had been found beside one of the dumpsters behind the dining hall. Like Elliot, he had been stripped naked and had the same ligature marks around the neck. However, unlike Elliot, none of the students standing around recognized the newest victim, which meant Hayden and his partner would have to positively identify the guy before they could officially link him to the Elliot case. But it was obvious to everyone that they were dealing with the same murderer. Shit. Headquarters was going to go nuts about this.

Samantha would be all over this new murder, too, Hayden thought as he pulled up beside the curb in front of Kendall's bookstore. She would look up at him with those big blue eyes of hers and think that if she sweet-talked him, he would give her all the inside information she wanted simply because he had a thing for her. Well, she'd be wasting her time, because there was no way in hell that he would be giving her anything. His mouth tightened. Except a good, sound spanking.

The bookstore was closed and dark inside, except for a slight glow of light coming from the back, but when Hayden peered in the window, he saw neither Kendall nor Samantha, not that he could see much of anything anyway. Which made him immediately wonder if she'd lied in her note. He clenched his jaw, irritated by the thought.

Swearing under his breath, Hayden made his way around to the back of the building, thinking that perhaps Kendall had asked Samantha to meet him there. But the back door was locked up tight as well.

Hayden was just about to leave when he noticed the car parked beside the curb. It had caught his attention not only because it was dark red, which was the color of the car that had almost run Samantha down at the Post, but also because it had a big scrape on the front passenger's side.

Hayden frowned. It could be a coincidence, he supposed, but his gut told him it wasn't. The damaged area on the car looked like it would line up perfectly with the paint smear that had been left on the support column in the newspaper parking garage.

Taking out his cell phone, he dialed the station. "Yeah, it's Tanner," he said. "I need you to run a plate for me."

After he gave the plate number, there was silence on the other end of the line for a few minutes. "Detective, it's registered to a Jack Kendall."

Kendall? Hayden's frown deepened at the name, but before he could even begin to make a correlation, a woman's scream came from inside the bookstore.

Hayden's blood ran cold. *Samantha.* "Shit," he muttered, his hand tightening on the cell phone. "I need back-up at The Bookstop on Meyer Street near the movie theater. Assault in progress."

Pulling his gun free from the holster, he ran to the back door of the bookstore and kicked it. It slammed back on its hinges and he held it open with his free hand while his eyes tried to penetrate the darkness.

That was when he heard Samantha scream again.

Samantha stared transfixed at the bookend in Jack Kendall's hand, trying to quell the fear rising within her. She thought of Hayden and of how angry he would be when he discovered that she'd gone off to investigate again. He'd probably spank her so hard that she wouldn't be able to sit down. If she ever saw the handsome detective again. Tears stung her eyes at the thought.

She threw a quick glance at the door. She had no doubt that she could get to it before Kendall, but then her heart sank as she remembered that he'd locked it with a key. There'd be no escape that way. A fresh wave of panic washed over her and she had to struggle not to give into her fear. She needed to keep a clear head if she was going to get out of this.

Perhaps if she tried talking to Kendall, she thought. Surely, she'd be able to reason with him. She took another step back, her hand stretched out before her in a placating gesture.

"Mr. Kendall, you really don't have to do this," she said, her voice trembling. "I can just forget what you told me. I mean, what you're doing – it's harmless, really. But murder...well, that would put you in prison for years. Life, even."

Something that looked like a smile touched his mouth. "The police will never be able to link your murder with me," he said, still walking toward her.

"But they will," she said quickly, taking a few more steps back, the movement bringing her even with a rack of books. "I left a note for my boyfriend saying that I was coming to see you."

That stopped him in his tracks for a moment, and then he shrugged. "When the cops ask, I'll tell them that, yes, you did come to see me, but that you left," he said. "Of course, I'll be very sorry to hear about what happened to you, Ms. Halliwell. I'll even make it look like your murder is connected to Rick's. That story you wrote for today's paper certainly had enough details to help with that."

Samantha saw his hand tighten around the bookend. Obviously, reasoning with Kendall wasn't going to work. She had to think of something else. And fast.

Abruptly, Kendall charged at her without warning, the heavy bookend raised high above his head.

Reaching out, she grabbed the only thing within reach, the desk lamp on the bookcase, and threw it at him, then turned and ran.

The lamp slowed Kendall down, but without the light coming from it, she could barely see anything in the store. She headed toward the back, desperately hoping there would be a door there that wasn't locked. But in the dark, she was at a distinct disadvantage. Kendall knew the store's layout; she didn't. She seemed to stumble over every chair and walk into every rack of books in the place while he was able to move quickly and easily. He beat her to what she assumed was the hallway that led to the back door and stood staring at her, bookend still in hand. He was breathing hard, but still looked determined.

She swept a pile of books and knickknacks off the nearest shelf and into his path, then whirled around and ran back the way she'd come, overturning racks of books and chairs as she went. It slowed him down a little bit, but not enough. As she reached the steps that led to the upper level, he was on her again, slamming into her and knocking her to the floor.

Turning onto her back, she kicked out with her foot and felt it thump against something solid. There was a grunt and Kendall fell backward a few steps. Heart pounding in her chest, she quickly pushed herself to her feet. But she didn't even get more than a few steps before Kendall threw himself at her legs. They both went down in a tumble.

Samantha twisted around just in time to see Kendall lifting the bookend. She let out a scream, kicking and flailing in desperation. Her foot caught Kendall in the stomach and he fell back with a grunt of pain. She yanked her legs out from under him and scrambled to her feet.

She fled up the steps, stumbling in her haste. She made it the top, but not fast enough. Kendall caught up with her, grabbing her arm and spinning her around. Samantha lashed out at him with her fists. All it would take was one blow from the heavy bookend to put an end her struggles.

"Samantha!"

Relief coursed through Samantha at the sound of Hayden's voice.

"Hayden!" she yelled, struggling against Kendall with renewed strength now. "I'm up here! Help!"

Kendall muttered something under his breath, his grip on her arm tightening, and Samantha held her breath. But then he hesitated, as if unsure what to do. It was enough to give Hayden the time he needed to get up the stairs and pull the bookstore owner away from her.

Hayden flung the man violently against the railing. Kendall landed on the floor with a thud. He lay there for a moment as if deciding whether he should try and make a run for it, but apparently Hayden wasn't going to give him the chance.

Lifting his gun, he aimed it at the other man's chest. "Don't even think about moving," he growled.

Samantha leaned against the railing, trembling as she watched Hayden jerk Kendall's arms behind his back and handcuff him to the wooden rail. He was saying something about the bookstore owner being under arrest, but her heart was pounding so loudly that she could barely hear the words.

Then Hayden was at her side, his gentle hands on her shoulders.

"Are you okay? Did he hurt you?" he asked. He had to bend slightly so that he could see her face and when she looked up, she saw that his was filled with concern.

She swallowed hard and opened her mouth to tell him that she was, but she couldn't seem to make the words come out. Tears welled in her eyes. Swearing under his breath, Hayden pulled her into his arms. She clung to him, burrowing her face into his chest. She didn't think she'd ever be able to find words to tell him how grateful she was that he'd found her.

Hayden gently stroked her hair. "*Shh*," he said softly. "You're safe now, sweetheart. Kendall can't hurt you."

Samantha lifted her head to look up at him. "You found my note?" was all she could say.

Hayden nodded. "What happened, Samantha?" he asked gently.

She glanced at Kendall. He was slumped with his back against the railing, ignoring her and Hayden.

She sniffed and turned back to Hayden. "It's stupid, really," she said in a trembling voice. "He said he had information about Rick Elliot's murder, so he asked me to meet him here. He seemed like such a harmless, old man, but it turns out that he's nothing more than a petty criminal. He's selling stripped books." When Hayden shook his head in confusion, she elaborated. "It's when bookstores take the covers off books and report them as unsold to the publisher. They're supposed to destroy them, but Kendall was selling them. He was so paranoid about getting caught that he lured me here to kill me just so he wouldn't lose his stupid bookstore."

Her voice trailed off, tears welling in her eyes again, and Hayden pulled her back into his arms. "He couldn't have lured you here if you had done as I told you, Samantha."

She winced at his tone. While Hayden's arms were still comforting, there was no mistaking the anger in his voice. He was probably right, but there was no way she was going to let him know that. She took a step back and wiped the last of the tears off her cheek. "I already told you, he said that he had information about Rick Elliot. I'm a reporter and it's my job to find out what he knew."

From the way Hayden's jaw tightened, she knew that he wanted to respond, but several uniform cops came into the bookstore just then and he was forced to turn his attention back to Kendall.

Samantha picked up her shoulder bag from where she had dropped it on the floor and took out her spiral notebook and a pen. She forced herself to focus. A story had just fallen into her lap and she needed to take notes while it was all fresh in her mind.

Hayden, of course, didn't see it that way. It took him a while to get everything straight with the uniforms, and then he had to go over the whole thing again when a patrol sergeant showed up. When he finally got Kendall into a squad car and on his way, he moved to her side.

"What are you doing?" he demanded.

She glanced up at him. "Taking notes for my story."

"Kendall almost killed you, Samantha, and you're standing here taking notes so you can write some ridiculous story?" he asked incredulously.

She bristled at that. "It's only ridiculous to you, Hayden; to everyone else it's news. And the story's all mine."

An officer came over just then, saying he needed to speak to Hayden. His mouth tightened at the interruption. "We'll talk about this when we get home," he said to her, his voice soft and controlled, as if he were barely keeping his anger in check.

Which meant that he would be spanking her when they got back to his apartment, she thought bitterly.

Samantha took a perverse sort of pleasure at the idea of making Hayden wait while she asked one of the officers a few more questions, but seeing the dark look on his face, she quickly closed her notebook. They left the bookstore to ride back to his apartment in stony silence. Samantha considered trying to get him to see the logic of her position, but a quick look at Hayden's clenched jaw and she decided against it. She was a reporter and Hayden was just going to have to learn to deal with that, she thought, but that argument was going to have to wait until he calmed down.

He didn't seem to be angry when they reached the apartment. Instead, he seemed completely calm, in a stern sort of way. As soon as they got in the door, he motioned her toward the living room, where he stood with arms folded while he glared down at her, looking every inch the police officer reprimanding a wayward miscreant.

When he finally spoke, she could hear the controlled anger in his voice. "What the hell were you thinking, Samantha, meeting Kendall like that?" he demanded.

She lifted her chin. "I told you. He said that he had some information about Elliot. How was I supposed to know he was going to try to kill me?"

"Gee, I don't know," he said sarcastically. "The fact that he wanted you to come to his bookstore in the middle of the night, perhaps?"

She shrugged. "I didn't think –"

He swore under his breath. "That's your problem, Samantha, you don't think!" he snapped. "You run off to investigate a lead on a murder case without even considering that it could be dangerous just because you want some stupid story." He raked his hand through his hair in frustration. "Dammit, Samantha! If you hadn't left a note or I hadn't gone looking for you..."

Samantha's heart squeezed in her chest at the anguish in his voice. He really cared about her, she realized. "I'm sorry," she said in a small voice.

His expression hardened. "Sorry isn't good enough, Samantha. If I can't trust you to use your own good judgment, then I'll make sure that next time, you do as I tell you."

Without another word, he grasped her arm, took a seat on the couch and dragged her over his knee.

She tried to push herself upright. "Hayden, wait..."

But he ignored her protest. Holding her firmly in place with his arm, he pushed up her skirt with his free hand, and then yanked down her panties to expose her bare bottom. He didn't stop to admire her curves like he had when he'd put her over his knee earlier, but immediately started in on her spanking.

Samantha gasped and cried out, amazed at how much the smacks stung. Shouldn't he at least give her a warm-up first? But apparently, those first couple of smacks were a warm-up because as his hand came down over and over on her ass, the spanks got harder and harder.

She struggled against him, desperately trying to free herself. But he only tightened his grip around her waist and continued to lecture her about how foolish she'd been as he brought his hand down on her already stinging asscheeks again and again.

"*Owww!* Hayden, that stings!" she whimpered.

Her bottom felt like it was on fire! Yet, in spite of how fiercely the spanks stung, her pussy was getting as wet it had when he'd spanked her in his kitchen earlier. Her face turned red. How could she possibly be getting excited? she wondered. And she wasn't the only one, she realized. She could feel Hayden's hard cock pressing against her hip. The thought that he was just as turned on by spanking her as she was by getting spanked was enough to make her pussy spasm.

"Hayden, please…" she begged. If he didn't stop spanking her soon, she was going slide her hand into her panties and touch herself. "I've learned my lesson. I'll be more careful. I promise!"

Samantha didn't know if it was the entreaty in her voice or that Hayden had simply decided she'd been punished enough, but whatever the reason, he stopped spanking her. She started to sigh with relief, only to jump when she felt his hand on her ass. But he only began to gently rub the sting from her cheeks. She let out a little moan as he gave her bottom a squeeze. Mmm, that was nice.

She cooed and lifted her ass higher, silently begging him for more. As if reading her mind, he slipped his hand between her legs to lightly run his fingers along he slick folds of her pussy. She spread her legs, offering even more of herself to him. Finding her throbbing clit, he gently began to caress the little nub with his finger.

Samantha drew in a sharp breath, and then let out a sound that was half sigh, half moan as she writhed against his hand. He slowly moved his finger in a rhythmic circle, first one way and then the other, back and then forth, until she was panting with the sheer ecstasy of it.

"Come for me, baby," Hayden said softly.

Samantha obeyed, coming harder than she'd ever thought possible. Her orgasm started at her clit, and then moved outward so that pleasure was coursing through her entire body. She cried out with the intensity of it, not caring if the whole apartment building heard her.

When her orgasm had subsided, Samantha lay limply over his lap for a moment, too spent to do more than that. Hayden slowly ran his finger along her folds again, this time gently sliding into her pussy. She caught her breath and held it for a moment, then let out quick little pants of pleasure as he moved his finger in and out of her wetness.

Samantha could have had him do that all night. But apparently, Hayden had other things in mind because he slid his finger out and gently urged her up from his lap.

She kneeled beside him on the couch, looking at him from beneath lowered lashes. Without a word, Hayden slid his hand into her hair and covered her mouth with his. She leaned into him, her fingers finding the buttons on his shirt. After foreplay like that she was more than ready for the main event.

Hayden must have had the same idea because he slid his hands underneath the hem of her top. She lifted her arms so he could take it off, but then quickly went back to undoing the buttons on his shirt. Or at least she tried to. Her fingers, however, didn't seem to want to cooperate. Hayden must have noticed her frustration because he chuckled and quickly stripped off his shirt.

Samantha could only sit back and stare at his chiseled chest and washboard stomach. Damn, he was delicious.

She would have been content to just sit there and gaze at him for a while, but again Hayden had other ideas. She didn't complain as he pulled her close for another kiss, though. Or when she felt him reach around to unhook her bra. Her breasts spilled into his waiting hands and she murmured her approval against his mouth as he gave her nipples a gentle squeeze.

Just as eager to touch him, she ran her hands over his muscular chest and down his six-pack abs. Grasping his belt buckle, she gave it a tug, and then went to work on the buttons of his jeans. She didn't have nearly as many problems with them as she had the ones on his shirt, but since Hayden was sitting down, she needed his assistance to get his jeans off. While he did that, she took the opportunity to wiggle out of her skirt. As Hayden's thick, hard cock came into view, she stared, mesmerized by how perfect he was. She was tempted to lean forward and take him in her mouth, but before she could move, Hayden took her hand and pulled her on top of him to straddle his lap.

Samantha rested her hands on his shoulder and positioned herself above his cock. Hayden teased with the head for a moment, but then, as if unable to hold back any longer, he slid inside her in one swift motion. Samantha gasped and clutched his broad shoulders, amazed at how completely he filled her pussy. She'd never been with a man who fit her so perfectly.

Hayden pressed his mouth the curve of her neck. "Ride me, Samantha," he entreated softly, his hands sliding up her smooth legs to firmly cup her freshly-spanked ass.

She obeyed the command without hesitation, moving up and down on his hard length. Her ass was still warm and tingling from the spanking he'd given her, and his touch made her gasp aloud.

"Hayden..." she breathed, lowering her head to kiss him.

"Come for me, baby," he whispered against her lips, his voice hoarse with need.

Again, Samantha obeyed, riding him faster and faster until she reached her peak, coming so hard that she thought she would pass out from the ecstasy of it.

Hayden's own release quickly followed, his hoarse groans echoing her cries of pleasure as he poured his cum into her.

Afterward, Samantha collapsed on top of him, her head on his shoulder, her long, blond hair covering his bare chest. Long minutes passed before either one could speak.

"Hayden..." she said softly. "I really am sorry about going to see Kendall."

Hayden said nothing.

"You were right," she continued quietly. "It was a stupid thing to do and I should have been more careful."

Still, he said nothing. She chewed on her lower lip, wondering if she should just let it go. But she couldn't.

"You would have done the same thing if Kendall had told you that he had information about the case," she pointed out.

For a moment, Samantha thought he still wasn't going to say anything, but then he finally spoke.

"Probably," he agreed quietly. "But that's different. I'm a..."

She drew back to look at him. "Don't you dare say it's because you're a man."

His mouth quirked at the indignation in her voice. "I was going to say that it's different because I'm a cop who has a lot more experience dealing with low-lifes like Kendall."

She bit her lip, but said nothing, and he reached out to gently cup her face with his hand. "Promise me that you won't do anything like that again, Samantha."

She hesitated for a moment. She knew that as a reporter, she probably shouldn't make those kinds of promises, but in spite of the fact that she'd been the one to bring up the subject, things were so perfect right now that she didn't want to spoil it.

"I promise," she said softly.

"Good." Hayden slid his hand in her hair to pull her close for another kiss. "Then no more talk about the case."

That was fine with Samantha.

Sweeping her up in his arms, he got to his feet and carried her into the bedroom. They made love again, but this time more slowly, and as Samantha curled up in Hayden's arms and drifted off to sleep, she found herself thinking that it would be very easy to fall for the handsome police detective.

Chapter Five

Samantha awoke to a ringing alarm clock the next morning. Still half asleep, she stirred slowly, but by the time she could talk herself into getting up to turn it off, a man's strong arm reached out to do it for her, and she remembered where she was.

Hayden encircled her waist with his arm and pulled her back against the hard wall of his chest to nuzzle the curve of her neck. His mouth was warm on her skin and she shivered.

"I've got to get up and go to work," he said. His voice was soft and husky with sleep, and filled with more than a touch of regret.

She looked out the window and saw that the sun was just beginning to come up. She snuggled back against him. "But it's barely light out," she protested, burrowing deeper into the pillow.

He chuckled softly and lowered his head to kiss the curve of her neck again. Beneath the blanket, his hand found its way over her hip and down her stomach to the soft curls between her legs, and when he slid his finger along the folds of her pussy, she moaned and turned onto her back, fully awake now.

"What about work?" she asked, giving him a teasing look.

His mouth quirked. "I'll skip breakfast," he said, leaning forward to kiss her.

Samantha moaned, her arms going up to wrap around his neck. She could definitely get used to waking up like this, she thought as tongue swept into her mouth to tease hers.

His hand glided over her leg and up her tummy to cup her breast. Taking her between his thumb and forefinger, he gave it a gentle squeeze. She sighed against his mouth.

"Do you like that?" he asked softly.

"*Mmm-hmmm,*" she breathed.

"And how about this?"

As he spoke, he trailed kisses along her neck and down to her breasts, pushing the blanket down as he went. Taking a nipple in his mouth, he gently suckled on it while he slid his free hand between her legs. Samantha moaned as his fingers found her clit and began to make slow, rhythmic circles. She arched against his hand, rotating her hips in time with his movements.

With a groan, Hayden released her nipple to slowly kiss his way down her stomach. Samantha followed his movements with her gaze, breathless with anticipation. The closer he got to the juncture of her thighs, the faster her pulse raced, and she couldn't stifle her cry of pleasure when she finally felt his tongue on her clit.

Wanting to keep his mouth right where it was, she lifted her hand and buried her fingers in his hair. Hayden didn't seem to kind, though. Instead, he cupped her bottom with both hands and made slow, little circles on her clit with his tongue.

Damn, he was talented at that. Within moments, he had her writhing on the bed and screaming out in ecstasy as he brought her to one orgasm after another.

Only when he had coaxed every bit of pleasure from her did Hayden kiss his way back up her body and position himself between her legs. He braced himself on his strong arms for a moment before sliding inside her. As he filled her pussy, Samantha pulled him down for a kiss, her arms and legs going around him as he slowly began to thrust in and out.

As good as what he was doing felt, though, she needed more. "Harder," she demanded, dragging her mouth away from his.

At her command, Hayden buried his face in the curve of her neck and began to pump his hips faster and faster until the whole bed was shaking.

Pleasure coursed through Samantha and she threw back her head and cried out, her screams so loud that she barely even heard Hayden's hoarse groans. Somehow, she did, though, and knowing that he was coming with her only made her own orgasm that much stronger.

It was a long time before Hayden lifted his head, and when he did it was to look at her with those soulful dark eyes of his. "You're incredible, do you know that?"

Samantha blushed. "You're pretty incredible yourself," she said, pulling him down for a kiss.

Hayden lifted his head with a groan. "Now I really do have to get up and go to work," he said. Lowering his head, he kissed her lingeringly on the mouth once more before getting out of bed.

Samantha lay back against the pillows, watching as he moved around the room naked and not a bit self-conscious. Not that he needed to be, she thought appreciatively, taking in his well-muscled legs and great ass.

"I'm going to take a quick shower," he said, and then gave her a lopsided smile. "I'd ask you to join me, but if I did, I'd never get to work."

A smile curved her lips as she lay listening to Hayden shower in the adjoining bathroom. Last night, she'd told herself that it would be easy to fall for him, but now, in the clear light of day, she decided that she already had. It seemed incredible, especially since she couldn't even stand him when they'd first met, but what else could that funny fluttery feeling in her tummy be, if not love?

Hayden came back into the bedroom before she could explore her thoughts further. His hair was still damp from the shower, and as she watched him get dressed, she couldn't help but think how delicious he looked.

"You can stay in bed, you know," he said, glancing at her as he reached for a shirt.

She shook her head. "I need to get to the paper."

He frowned at that, but made no comment, other than, "I'll drop you off."

Completely dressed, Hayden came back over to where she still sat on the bed and kissed her. "I'm going to put on coffee if you want some."

She smiled and nodded, and he gazed down at her for a moment before kissing her again – a slow kiss that made her tingle right down to the tips of her toes.

Leaning back against the pillows with a sigh, Samantha watched him walk from the room. Well, if she wasn't in love, then she was in really deep like – or lust, she decided, thinking how amazing the sex with him was. No man had ever left her as breathless – or made her feel as beautiful – as Hayden did.

No man had ever spanked her, either, she thought with a smile. She never would have imagined that spanking could be such an incredible turn on. It was enough to make her think she'd have to get herself into trouble on a regular basis.

Stretching her arms over her head, she threw back the sheet and got out of bed only to realize that her clothes were still in the living room. She supposed she could be as self-possessed as Hayden and walk into the kitchen stark naked, but she didn't think she could be that bold just yet.

She considered for a moment, and then decided that Hayden probably wouldn't mind if she borrowed one of his shirts. Padding across the room on bare feet, she walked over to the closet and picked out a button-up shirt, then went into the bathroom to take a quick shower. After drying off, she took a minute to run her fingers through her hair before slipping on Hayden's shirt. It was big on her, but soft and comfortable, and she decided that there was something very sexy about wearing her lover's shirt.

Samantha heard the soft murmur of voices as she walked into the living room. At first, she thought it was the television, but then she recognized Hayden's voice and realized he had a visitor.

Though their voices were coming from the kitchen, there was no way she could dart into the living room and get her clothes without being seen. She was about to turn and go back into the bedroom when their conversation made her stop.

"Bauer was pre-med, though," a man was saying.

Samantha frowned. She didn't recognize the name, but there was something in the man's tone that made her think it was important. She waited for the man to say more, but it was Hayden who spoke. His voice was too soft for her to hear and she took a few steps closer to peek around the doorjamb cautiously. Though she didn't know his name, she recognized the man. He was Hayden's partner.

"I talked to the ME on the way over here," he said to Hayden. "We got lucky. The killer left something for us."

"Did he say...?"

Hayden's voice trailed off abruptly as he caught sight of Samantha. She flushed guiltily, feeling like she'd just been caught with her hand in the cookie jar. Not only had she been eavesdropping, but now his partner would know she had spent the night. Knowing she'd look like an idiot if she darted back into the bedroom, she walked the rest of the way into the kitchen.

"Samantha, this is my partner, Nik Sullivan."

Hayden's voice sounded odd, and Samantha wondered if he were angry that she'd been listening in on their conversation, or simply embarrassed that his partner had found them together.

"Nik, Samantha Halliwell."

Nik glanced briefly at Hayden, and then held out his hand. "The reporter from the other day, right?" Nik said, glancing at Hayden again.

She nodded. "It's nice to meet you." She glanced at Hayden, too, and saw that he looked uncomfortable. "There's been another murder?" she asked, her gaze going back to Nik.

Awkward silence followed her words, during which Nik looked at Hayden, who cleared his throat.

"I'll see you at the station," he told his partner.

Nik gave Samantha a nod. "It was nice meeting you," he told her.

"Why didn't you tell me there'd been another murder?" she asked Hayden after Nik had left.

Hayden poured coffee into a mug and held it out to her. "I had other things on my mind last night, Samantha, if you'll remember."

She blushed and busied herself with adding cream and sugar to her coffee. "So, is it the same MO?" she asked after a moment.

He hesitated for a moment, then said, "Yeah."

She nodded. "Have you been able to link him to Elliot?"

He took a swallow of coffee. "Not yet, but we do know he was a student. That's off the record, of course."

"Of course," she agreed. "I heard your partner say he was pre-med. No obvious link to Elliot there." She thought a moment, and then put her mug down on the counter, her coffee untouched. "I need to get going. I'm already behind on the story for this new murder and I still have to write about Kendall."

As she spoke, she walked into the living room and started picking up her clothes from where they'd been tossed on the couch. Frowning, Hayden watched her for a moment before following.

"Wait a minute, Samantha," he said, putting his hand on her arm. "I don't want you getting yourself into trouble again."

She looked up at him innocently. "I'm not going to get myself into trouble," she said, and then smiled. "Besides, if I do, I'm sure you'll come to my rescue. Then spank me, of course, for being so irresponsible," she added, blushing even as she said the words.

Despite the fact that he was angry with her for making light of the whole thing, he felt himself go hard at the thought spanking her again. "I'm serious, Samantha," he said gruffly, determined to remain focused on the conversation. "First, there was the guy at the bar, and then Kendall..."

She shrugged. "But you're right, I've learned my lesson." Hayden lifted a brow and she sighed. "Look, I'm just going to go to the university and ask some questions. I'm not looking to ferret out the killer, I'm just looking to get a story."

Hayden would have put her over his knee right then if he thought it would have done any good, but Samantha was so determined to get a story that he suspected the only way to keep her from going after it would be to handcuff her to the bed. As appealing as that was, he'd rather save the handcuffs for something more pleasurable.

He could only think of one way to keep her from meddling in the really dangerous part of this investigation. But to do that, he would have to do something he swore he'd never do again.

Putting his hands on her shoulders, he gazed down at her, his expression earnest. "I'll give you whatever information about the case that I can, Samantha, but you have to promise me that you won't do anything to put yourself in danger," he said.

She hesitated for a moment. "Define putting myself in danger," she said slowly.

His brows drew together warningly and she hurried to appease him.

"Okay, okay. I promise," she said.

He regarded her thoughtfully for a moment. "Good," he said, and then lowered his head to kiss her.

She leaned into him, kissing him back, and he let out a groan.

"You should get dressed," he said, releasing her reluctantly.

She nodded and turned to go back into the bedroom, but he caught her hand and brought her back around. "You look sexy as hell in that shirt, you know."

She smiled and gave him a look that was so damn sexy it took everything in him not to follow her into the bedroom and make love to her again.

He just hoped that by trusting her he wasn't making the biggest mistake of his life.

Samantha asked Hayden to drop her at her apartment so she could grab a change of clothes.

"My roommate can give her a ride to the paper," she said.

Though he wouldn't have minded waiting, he needed to get to work, and so he agreed. While they drove to her place, he shared what he knew about the newest victim, which wasn't much, but at the door, he promised to update her with whatever he learned.

Hayden found Nik sitting at his desk when he got to the station. His partner looked up from whatever it was he'd been reading, an amused look on his face.

"Don't say it," Hayden warned before his friend could speak.

Nik chuckled. "Say what? I was the one who told you that not every reporter is like Jessica."

Hayden's face darkened into a scowl as he sat down. "Samantha's nothing like Jessica," he said sharply.

His partner regarded him thoughtfully for a moment. "Who are you trying to convince, Hayden, me or yourself?"

Hayden's frown deepened, but he said nothing. Samantha wasn't like Jessica, he told himself. She was a reporter who wanted a story, that was true, but unlike Jessica, Samantha wasn't using him to get it. At least, he didn't think she was.

"Look, don't overanalyze it, Hayden," Nik suggested, interrupting his thoughts. "You obviously like Samantha, but you're afraid to trust her because she's a reporter. She could also be the best thing that ever happened to you, and if you call it quits, you'll be kicking yourself for the rest of your life."

Hayden glared at him. "Thank you, Dr. Phil," he said sarcastically.

Nik shrugged. "I'm just saying."

Hayden said nothing in reply, forcing his mind off Samantha and onto the case.

"So, what did the ME find?" he asked.

"A female pubic hair," Nik said.

Hayden thought a moment. "It could be from the same woman who was involved with Elliot."

Nik shrugged, but Captain Conner came up to them before he could answer. He looked from one detective to the other.

"Where are we on the university murders?" he asked, and then nodded when Nik told him about the ME's findings.

"So, we're back to this mystery woman, who might or might not be a link to Elliot. Well, at least now we know that she's a brunette," Conner said. "Get over to the university and start digging around about this new vic. See if we can find a link between him and Elliot. If we're lucky, maybe someone will remember seeing him with her. It's not much, but right now we have nothing else to go on. We'll wait for the DNA, but I'll bet my paycheck that it won't match anything in the system. While you two are over at the college, I'll have Mason work up a profile on NCIC and VICAP. From the MO, I'd say this isn't the first time the killer has done this."

Hayden had to agree, which meant that the murderer was going to be extremely adept at covering his tracks. He would also likely move to a new area if he thought the cops were closing in on him.

Samantha's roommate had been only too happy to drop her at the newspaper on her way to work. Mostly because Alexa wanted the dish on the handsome detective.

At the Post, Samantha got to work on her story about Kendall and his stripped books before using the information Hayden had given her to do a write-up on the newest murder victim, Jeffrey Bauer. After that, she headed to the university. Remembering that the registrar had helped her out before, she stopped to grab a cup of coffee and a danish for the woman, thinking that a little bribe couldn't hurt.

It didn't, and Samantha walked out of the registrar's office with not only a list of Jeffrey Bauer's classes, but also a list of the students in those classes, as well as each of their class schedules. She compared his classes against the list she had for Rick Elliot, only to discover that they'd had none of the same classes. Not that she'd thought they would, seeing as Elliot's major had been art history, while Bauer had been pre-med. He had the classes to prove it, too, she thought. Anatomy and physiology, organic chemistry, physics, biochemistry. She got a headache just thinking about all that science.

Knowing that she'd learn more from the university's students than she would from staring at a computer printout, she headed over to the student union. The university had held a memorial for Jeffrey Bauer that morning, and judging by the abundance of flowers that had been placed around the area they'd set aside for honoring the murdered student, Bauer had been just as well liked as Elliot.

With a sigh, Samantha walked up the steps and went into the student union, where a good portion of the university's students had gathered. Pushing her sunglasses up on her head, she took out her spiral notebook and a pen, then made her way over to a group of students that were sitting around a low coffee table.

They looked up at her approach and she quickly introduced herself. "I'm Samantha Halliwell from the Post, and I was wondering if I could ask you a few questions about Jeffrey Bauer."

One of the guys gave her a shrug and a nod. He was short and solidly built with dark, curly hair. "Yeah, I guess."

"My roommate dated him for a while," a slim, blond girl said quietly.

Samantha waited for her to say more, but the girl fell silent. "What happened with that?"

"She wanted to be exclusive, Jeff didn't."

Samantha nodded. "Do you know who he'd been currently seeing?"

It was one of the guys who answered. "You could talk to Sean Radcliff. He was pretty tight with Jeff."

Samantha wrote down the name. "Do you know where I can find him?"

He gestured to a table full of guys that was across the room. "The guy in the red shirt."

Samantha thanked them and made her way over to the other table just as the guys were getting to their feet.

"Sean Radcliff?"

They all looked up at the name, but it was the guy in the red shirt who nodded. "Yeah, I'm Sean."

"I'm Samantha Halliwell from the Post. I was wondering if I could ask you a few questions about Jeffrey Bauer."

He hesitated for a moment, and then glanced at the other guys. "I'll catch up with you," he said, and then pulled out a chair and sat down.

Samantha did the same. "I heard that you and Jeff were friends. I'm sorry about what happened."

He nodded. "What did you want to know about him?"

"Actually, I wanted to know if he'd been seeing anyone," she said.

A wry smile touched his mouth. "Jeff was always seeing someone."

She nodded. "But was there a particular girl he talked about?"

Sean shook his head. "Not really," he said, but then a frown creased his forehead. "Though there was this one girl..."

"What about her?" Samantha prompted.

He shrugged. "I don't know, really. Jeff would never talk about her. He never brought her back to the dorm either, which I thought was odd. I was starting to think she was underage or something."

She thought a moment. "Did Jeff know Rick Elliot?"

"The other guy who was murdered?"

She nodded.

"Jeff never mentioned him." He glanced at his watch, and then gave her an apologetic look. "I got to be somewhere."

"Of course," she said. "Thank you."

Well, Samantha thought as she nibbled on the top of her pen, whether Rick Elliot and Jeffrey Bauer knew each other or not, they certainly had one thing in common. A mystery woman. It was too big of a coincidence; it had to be the same woman. But, who was she?

"I should put you over my knee, Samantha, and spank you right here."

Hayden's voice, soft as velvet next to her ear, sent ripples of desire running through her, and despite the fact that no on else in the student union could possibly have heard what he'd said, she blushed.

"Hayden!" she said, her voice breathless, her bottom tingling at the mere mention of a spanking. Turning her head slightly, she found him leaning over her chair, one hand on the back, the other on the table.

"I thought you were going to behave yourself," he said, pulling out the chair and sitting down beside her.

She gave him what she thought was sure to be an innocent look. "What do you mean?"

"I mean that you should be at the paper working on your story, not here investigating this case."

"I wasn't investigating the case," she told him. "I'm just getting some human interest stuff on the guys that were murdered. Just background, nothing dangerous. No snooping involved."

Hayden's mouth quirked. If he didn't know her better, he'd almost believe her. Well, at least she wasn't questioning some guy in a dark alley or meeting a homicidal bookstore owner in the middle of the night. That was something, he supposed.

"I did learn something very interesting, though," she continued before he could say anything, and then related what Sean Radcliff had told her, adding that she thought the murderer could be this mystery woman.

Hayden frowned, but said nothing.

"What is it?" she asked.

He shook his head. "Nothing, just something the ME found."

She waited for him to say more and when he remained silent, she prompted him. "So, what did he find?"

He hesitated. "Nothing that you can put in your story."

She shrugged. "Off the record, then."

He regarded her thoughtfully. He wanted to trust her, part of him even did, but the last time he'd trusted a reporter with privileged information, it had almost cost him his job. Samantha wasn't Jessica, deep down he knew that. He also knew that the only way he would ever come to trust Samantha was to just take that leap of faith. So, he took a deep breath and told her about the biggest lead they had in the case, the female pubic hair.

"Interesting." She probably would have said more, but he quickly turned the conversation back to her before she could press him further.

"So, are you going back to the paper?" he asked.

She nodded. "In a bit," she said, and then smiled at him. "Will I see you later?"

The corner of his mouth curved. "I'll probably be working on the case pretty late, but I could come by your place after I get off."

Samantha ran her tongue over her lips – an unconscious gesture, he was sure – and Hayden felt himself go hard. What was it about her that got him so aroused? They'd made love just a few hours ago and already he wanted her again.

"You can't imagine how much I want you right now..." he said, his voice husky with desire.

She blushed, and it was all he could do not to lean forward and kiss her. Clearing his throat, he glanced around the room and saw his partner questioning a pair of students that were sitting at a nearby table. Turning back to Samantha, Hayden gave her a rueful smile.

"I should get going."

She nodded and he stood, but then bent over her chair again. "Remember, behave yourself, Samantha," he said softly in her ear. "Or I really will have to spank you."

Samantha's pulse skipped a beat, and as she watched Hayden walk across the room to stand beside his partner, she found herself wondering what she would do if Hayden had decided that she should be spanked right there and then. She felt herself flush at the image, and her color only deepened as that image became a full-fledged erotic fantasy.

In it, Hayden stood before her, his arms folded while he scolded her for continuing to investigate the case.

"Especially when I repeatedly told you not to," he said sternly.

"But I wasn't investigating," she protested. "It was just some human interest stuff for my story."

He smirked. "Nice try, Samantha," he said, and with that, he took her hand and pulled her gently to her feet.

But she hung back, wary. "What are you doing?"

"I'm going to spank you."

"But you can't," she protested, looking around the crowded student union. "Not in front of all these people. What will they think!"

Lifting her chin with his finger, he bent his head and slowly kissed her on the mouth. "They'll think that you've been a bad girl," he told her, his voice husky.

But as he had her bend over the table, and then lifted her skirt to expose her panty-clad bottom, she was surprised to see that no one in the student union even looked their way. Not even when Hayden began spanking her.

He started gently, lightly smacking one cheek, and then the other, before gradually increasing the intensity until she was letting out "oh's!" and "ow's!" of protest.

Then Hayden's hands were slowly sliding down her delicate panties and those soft cries of protest became a moan of pleasure as he caressed her heated skin. Which quickly turned into a gasp of surprise as he started spanking her again.

He soon had her wiggling and shifting from one foot to the other, but she obediently held her position, gripping the edges of the table tightly while he continued spanking her.

Abruptly, he stopped to admire his handiwork and she let out a sigh of pleasure as he gently ran his hand over her hot skin.

"You're bottom is so red," Hayden said softly. "But not red enough, I think."

Behind her, she heard him undoing his belt, heard the whisper of the leather as he slid it from the loops, and she held her breath. He wouldn't, she thought, but a quick look over her shoulder saw him doubling it in his hand, and she knew that he most definitely would!

She held her breath, her pulse racing, only to let out an "*oh!*" of surprise as the belt slapped against her already well-spanked behind. Before she could even take a breath, it slapped against her skin again, and she let out another "*oh!*" then another and another as he spanked her again and again.

By the time he was finished, her bottom was glowing and she was incredibly excited. Not only in her fantasy, either, she realized as she felt the dampness between her thighs. But just as she imagined Hayden stepping up behind her, gripping her hips and sliding his cock deliciously deep inside her, a college student dropped his books on the table with a thud and sat down opposite her.

Samantha jumped, startled. She frowned at the interruption. With a sigh, she picked up her notebook and pen, shoved them in her shoulder bag and pushed back her chair. She should be getting back to the paper anyway.

Getting to her feet, she looked around the student union for Hayden, but didn't see him, and realized that he and his partner must have left while she'd been daydreaming.

Outside, two girls were standing by the flowers that had been left for Jeffrey Bauer, and as Samantha made her way past them, she couldn't help but overhear their conversation.

"First, Rick, and now Jeff," one of the girl's said quietly. "Do you think the killer is going after people in my class?"

Samantha stopped in her tracks. To her knowledge, Rick Elliot and Jeffrey Bauer didn't have any classes in common.

She turned back to the girls. "Excuse me," she said. "Did I hear you say that you had a class with Rick Elliot and Jeffrey Bauer?"

The girl who had spoken before nodded. "Yeah. Abnormal psychology."

Samantha frowned. She'd seen abnormal psychology listed on Rick Elliot's class schedule, but didn't remember seeing it on Jeffrey Bauer's. Could she have missed it? Reaching into her shoulder bag, she got out both lists and scanned them quickly. Sure enough, abnormal psychology was on Elliot's schedule, but not on Bauer's.

"Abnormal psychology with Dr. Capshaw?" Samantha asked and the girl nodded again. Samantha's brow furrowed. "I have Jeffrey Bauer's class schedule and abnormal psychology isn't listed."

The girl shrugged. "The professor let Jeff start after the drop/add period, so maybe that's why it's not on there."

Samantha considered that. "Were you friends with either Rick or Jeff?"

The girl tucked a strand of dark hair behind her ear. "Not really. Jeff asked me out, but I have a boyfriend, so I said no. Jeff was cool with it, though." A small smile curved her lips. "He asked out another girl in the class right afterward."

"Can I have her name?" Samantha asked.

The girl regarded her curiously. "Are you a cop?"

"A reporter. I'm doing a story."

The girl nodded. "Her name's Jill Novak."

Samantha wrote down the name and thanked the girls, who went inside the student union. Samantha thought about calling Hayden to tell him about this new lead, but then decided to check into it herself first. Though she wanted to talk to the girlfriend, she was thinking that perhaps this Dr. Capshaw would be able to shed some light on things as well. With that in mind, she headed for the professor's office.

Chapter Six

Dr. Capshaw's office was on the other side of campus, but since it was a beautiful day, Samantha decided to leave her car at the student union and walk.

The professor's office was in one of the newer buildings and seeing that the door was closed, she thought perhaps Dr. Capshaw was out, but when she knocked on the door, a man's voice asked her to come in.

Opening the door, she peered around it. "Dr. Capshaw?"

The man sitting at the desk looked up at her entrance. He was a handsome man in his mid-forties she guessed, with dark hair and hazel eyes that were regarding her curiously. "Yes?"

Samantha moved into the room. "I'm Samantha Halliwell from the Post," she said with a smile. "I'd like to talk to you about Rick Elliot and Jeffrey Bauer if I could. I understand they were students of yours."

He smiled. "Actually, you're looking for my wife. She's a professor here as well."

"Oh...do you know where I can find her?"

"Actually, we share an office," he said. "She should be back shortly. You're welcome to wait for her if you like."

He gestured to the couch that was against the opposite wall as he spoke, and Samantha sat. Putting her shoulder bag down beside her, she took out her notebook and a pen.

"It's awful what happened to those students," Dr. Capshaw said, sitting back in his chair.

She nodded. "Yes, it is."

He made no further comment and she took the opportunity to gaze around the room. There were a few posters depicting what she assumed were famous psychologists throughout history, though Freud was the only one she recognized. There was also a bulletin board with various notes tacked to it as well as a syllabus for each of the classes that he and his wife taught. On the opposite wall was a calendar that listed dates when projects were due and exams would be given.

"So, what is it that you teach?" she asked, turning back to him.

"Philosophy."

She thought a moment. She'd never taken a philosophy class in college, always opting for some other elective that had seemed more interesting. "You know, I've always wondered what one does with a philosophy degree."

He grinned. "Besides become a professor, you mean," he quipped, and she laughed. "Actually, philosophy gives you skills that you can use in almost any profession. If you have a philosophy degree, you can go into business, medicine, public relations, even journalism."

She regarded him skeptically. "Journalism?"

He shrugged. "Or law enforcement. Besides critical thinking and problem solving skills, reporters as well as police officers need to be able to distinguish between fact and fiction, all of which philosophy can teach."

Samantha wondered if Hayden would agree. Somehow, she couldn't picture the handsome detective spouting rhetoric, which was also something philosophy taught. But then again, he did seem to like telling her what to do, she thought with a smile.

Before she and the professor could continue their conversation, however, his wife walked in. She was tall and slim, and with her high cheekbones, brunette hair, and dark eyes, she was what some would call striking.

Dr. Capshaw got to his feet at his wife's entrance, and Samantha did the same.

78

"Miranda, this is Samantha Halliwell," he said, coming around the desk. "She's a reporter with the Post."

"I'd like to talk to you about the two students that were murdered," Samantha explained.

Miranda Capshaw shot her husband a nervous look before her gaze went back to Samantha. "I...I don't know what I can tell you."

If Dr. Capshaw noticed his wife's obvious unease, he gave no indication of it. "If you'll excuse me," he said, giving them both a nod.

Samantha waited until the philosophy professor had left the room before she spoke. "I understand that both Rick Elliot and Jeffrey Bauer were in your abnormal psychology class."

Miranda Capshaw wandered over to her desk and set down the textbook she'd been carrying. "Yes, that's right."

"I spoke to one of the other students in your class, and she told me that Jeff transferred in after the drop/add period," Samantha continued.

The woman straightened a stack of papers. "Jeff realized that he needed another psychology class. I had him in Psych 101 when he was a freshman and knew that since he was a good student, he'd have no problem catching up with the rest of the class."

Samantha nodded. "Did he?"

She shook her head. "Not at all. In fact, he was one of my best students."

"Was Rick Elliot a good student, too?"

Miranda Capshaw thought a moment, then shrugged. "Rick didn't have the same interest in psychology that Jeff had, but his grades were good."

"Were they friends, do you know?"

The professor shrugged again. "I suppose they could have been."

"Did you ever see them hang out together?"

"They talked in class, but I really couldn't say what they did outside of it."

Samantha thought a moment. "So, you wouldn't happen to know if either of them were dating any of the girls in your class?"

Miranda Capshaw looked at her sharply. "Do the police think a woman did it?"

Remembering her promise to Hayden that she would keep certain information off the record, Samantha chose her words carefully. "I don't really know what leads the police are investigating. The other students mentioned something about a girl both Rick and Jeff were seeing. I'm just following up on it. Do you know if either of them were seeing anyone in your class? Or someone outside of it, perhaps?"

Miranda Capshaw didn't answer. Instead, she was staring down at her desk, obviously deep in thought. Did she know something? Samantha wondered.

"Dr. Capshaw?"

The woman jumped a little, as if startled. "Oh...um, no, I don't know who they were going out with," she said quickly.

Samantha nodded and jotted her name and number down on a piece of notebook paper. "If you think of anything, would you let me know?" she asked.

Miranda Capshaw took the piece of paper Samantha held out to her. "Of course."

But the professor still looked uncomfortable, which made Samantha wonder again if the woman were withholding information. Maybe Dr. Capshaw was protecting the girl. Perhaps she should dig a little deeper, see if she could get the woman to talk. But then she remembered what had happened the last time she'd done some digging. If she put herself in danger again, the spanking Hayden had given her last night would probably look like a love pat compared to the spanking he'd give her if she got herself into trouble again. But that wasn't the thing that stopped her. On the contrary, the idea of being spanked for her misdeeds was more of a turn-on than a deterrent. No, what stopped her was the anguish her carelessness had caused Hayden. This time, she would mention her suspicions to Hayden and let him do the investigating.

Samantha glanced out the window as she reached for her shoulder bag, and saw that it had gotten dark and cloudy outside. "It looks like it wants to rain, and I left my car over at the student union," she said, putting away her notebook and pen. "I came across campus. Is there a shorter way back to the student union?"

Miranda Capshaw said nothing for a moment, obviously still preoccupied with her own thoughts, but then she nodded. "You can take the jogging path," she suggested. "It starts just behind this building. It's through the woods, but it's faster and brings you out behind the student union."

Samantha thanked her for both her time and the suggestion before leaving. In the hallway, she passed Miranda Capshaw's husband, who gave her a charming smile and told her to have a nice day.

As Samantha pushed open the door at the end of the hall, she happened to glance over her shoulder, and was surprised to see Dr. Capshaw looking at her. Or to be more precise, checking her out. Openly.

What a pig, she thought in disgust. The professor was a married man. Think he'd be more subtle.

"She knows, David," Miranda Capshaw told her husband when he walked in the door. "She knows we did it."

David Capshaw closed the door behind him, and then stood for a moment, regarding his wife in silence. She was chewing on her lower lip and wringing her hands, and looking more nervous than he'd ever seen her.

"How could she know?" he asked calmly.

Miranda shook her head. "Someone saw me with them."

He frowned. "Who?"

Her brow furrowed. "I don't know. But does it matter? David, she practically accused me! She knows they were both seeing the same woman, and she went round and round trying to get me to implicate myself. We have to leave. Now. Today."

He thought a moment, considering her words, and then shook his head. "If the papers are to be believed, then the police have no leads, and leaving will only arouse suspicion. It sounds like that reporter is just fishing for something."

She chewed on her lip. "But I saw her talking to one of those detectives in the student union this morning."

He shrugged. "So?"

"So, she's probably working with the police."

He snorted. "I doubt it. More likely, she was trying to get a story from them."

But Miranda still looked unconvinced. He put his hands on her shoulders. "Before we act, we need to find out exactly what this reporter knows, if anything, and whether she's told anyone. Then we can decide what to do next."

She looked up at him. "How are we going to find out what she knows?"

He shrugged. "It's not complicated, really. We simply need to ask her in the right way."

"You mean kidnap her?" she asked warily. "Isn't that risky? We've never dealt with anyone that didn't come with us willingly. What if someone sees us?"

"No one's going to see us." He trailed his finger down her cheek. "I heard you tell her about the jogging path. That was brilliant."

Miranda smiled. "But what do we do with her afterward?"

"I think that's obvious, don't you?"

"We've never killed a woman before," she said softly, as if she were intrigued by the idea.

David's mouth curved. "No, we haven't. But it could be fun, don't you think?"

"You know, I think it'd be easier to talk to the women that Jeffrey Bauer didn't date," Nik said. He shuffled the papers in his hand. "I mean, look at this. There've got be fifty names here. How'd the guy even have time for anything else?"

Hayden glanced at Nik briefly before focusing again on the road. They were on their way to a nearby coffee shop where one of Jeffrey Bauer's former girlfriends worked. They'd already spoken to a handful of other women since leaving the student union, but hadn't gotten anything useful.

"Do we even really think some college girl did these murders?" Nik asked.

Hayden shrugged his shoulders. "That, or some college girl's jealous boyfriend."

He would have said more, but his cell phone rang, interrupting him. Taking it from his pocket, he held it to his ear.

"Tanner."

"Hayden, it's Samantha."

"Hey," he said, a smile tugging on his mouth. "Are you back at the paper already?"

"Actually, I'm still at the university," she said. "I found a connection between Rick Elliot and Jeffrey Bauer. It turns out that they did have a class together. I talked to the professor and..."

Hayden waited for her to say more, and when she didn't, he frowned. "Samantha?"

Silence, and then a grating sound, like she had dropped the phone on the sidewalk or something.

"Samantha?" he said again.

More silence, and then a woman's scream.

Fear gripped him. "Shit," he muttered. He dialed her number quickly, but got no answer. "Double shit!"

Switching on the colored lights the car was equipped with, he flung a quick glance in the rearview mirror before doing a U-turn.

"What is it?" his partner asked as they sped toward the college.

Hayden's hand tightened on the wheel. "Samantha has this bad habit of sticking her nose where it doesn't belong, particularly when it comes to this murder investigation."

Quickly, he told his partner about Samantha's run-in with that creep in the alley outside The Dorm Room, and then her subsequent encounter with the bookstore owner.

"So, you think she stumbled onto something she shouldn't have over at the college?" Nik asked.

"I know she did." He slammed his hand against the steering wheel in frustration. "Dammit! She swore to me that she wouldn't put herself in danger again."

Hayden was suddenly short of breath. What if, this time, Samantha's snooping got her killed? He had just met her, and yet it seemed so right between them. Now...

He took a deep breath and let it out slowly, then chided himself. He had to get a grip.

Since Samantha had still been at the student union when he and Nik had left, Hayden decided to check there first. Her car, a VW Bug, was parked in the same spot that it had been before, but there was no sign of Samantha. He couldn't find any signs of a struggle at first, but then he noticed a cell phone in the grass near the curb. Swearing, he pulled out his own cell phone and dialed her number. A few seconds later, the phone he'd found began to ring.

"It's hers," he said to his partner.

He and Nik canvassed the area, but the more people he questioned, the more people shook their heads, and the more anxious he became.

Nik came up with nothing, either. "You want to call it in?" he asked.

"Yeah, we better. At least get people on the lookout for her. But we don't have a lot to go on."

While his partner reported the suspected kidnapping, Hayden stood and raked his hand through his hair in frustration, wondering what to do next. "Samantha said something about Rick Elliot and Jeffrey Bauer having a class together, even though it wasn't on their schedules, so whatever she stumbled upon, it must have to do with that. Hopefully, that will give us something to go on," he said as soon as his partner was off the phone. "We need to get over to the registrar."

But the registrar had no record of the two men having a class together.

"But that's impossible. I spoke with someone who told me they had a class together," Hayden insisted. "Isn't it possible that one of them added it after the semester started? Or maybe you just missed it."

The registrar, a plump, motherly-looking woman, shook her head. "The records are already updated with any drop/add's..." she began, but she must have seen the look of desperation on his face, because her voice trailed off. "I suppose we could have missed one. We keep the hard copies, though. You're welcome to look through them."

She walked across the room to a file cabinet and pulled open one of the drawers before turning to give Hayden and Nik an apologetic look. "They're not in alphabetical order, I'm afraid. But if either boy added a class, the drop/add form would be in here."

As she spoke, she took out a stack of papers, which she divided among Hayden, Nik, and herself. Taking his pile over to a nearby table, Hayden quickly began going through the forms. He was almost finished with his stack when the registrar spoke.

"Well, I'll be..." she said. "Jeffrey Bauer added abnormal psychology, but he did it after the drop/add period. I guess it must have gotten tossed in the drawer without being put on the computer."

Hayden was at her side immediately, the stack of papers he'd been looking through already forgotten.

"This professor, Miranda Capshaw," he said, reading the name off the form. "Where is her office?" he asked.

"Across campus, in the building beside the library," the woman told him.

Following the directions the registrar had given them, they headed over to Miranda Capshaw's office. This professor had to be the same one that Samantha had talked to, he thought, and whatever they had talked about must have gotten Samantha in trouble. But when he and Nik got to Dr. Capshaw's office, they found it locked, despite the fact that the schedule posted on the door said that her office hours were during that time.

"Shit!" Hayden swore.

Before he could say more, however, his cell phone rang. Desperately hoping it was Samantha, he yanked it from his pocket.

It wasn't Samantha, however, but Captain Conner wanting to know what was going on. Hayden quickly brought him up to speed with the connection between the two students, as well as Samantha's likely kidnapping. He was careful to keep any undo familiarity concerning Samantha out of his voice. He didn't want the captain pulling him off the search because of his relationship with her.

To his relief, the captain didn't seem to notice his anxiety. "That sounds about right. We found an MO match on NCIC. There've been matching MO's at seven different colleges and universities over the past ten years. Male students, strangled, and then dumped on the college campus. It could be a student or..."

Hayden's gaze strayed to Dr. Capshaw's office door. "Or a professor," he said slowly, finishing the thought.

"Exactly," Conner agreed. "What do we know about the professor that taught our two vics?"

"Right now, all we have is a name," Hayden told him. "She's not in her office."

"Any chance that she's the one who grabbed this reporter?"

"It's very likely. It's possible that she was at the professor's office minutes before she disappeared."

Conner was silent for a moment. "How'd you find out about this reporter being grabbed?"

Hayden fabricated something close to the truth. "I was on the phone with her. She was letting me know what she found out during her investigation. It's how I found out about the connection between the vics. It's probably what got her kidnapped."

Conner sighed. "Get an address on this professor. I'll start the warrant as soon as you get me the info. But don't wait for it to go in. I'll have tactical support meet you. The warrant will cover us for anything we find."

Hayden hung up and glanced at his partner before starting down the hallway. "Let's go."

Samantha awoke to find herself tied to a bed in a room she didn't recognize. Her head hurt something fierce and she squinted her eyes against the bright afternoon sun that was streaming through the window. What had happened? Where was she?

She'd taken the jogging path back to the student union as Miranda Capshaw had suggested, and was just walking across the parking lot when she'd decided to call Hayden. That was when someone had grabbed her.

She vaguely remembered dropping her cell phone before something had been tossed over her head and she was dragged, kicking and screaming, into a vehicle, where her captor had hit her hard enough on the side of the head to knock her unconscious.

But now that she was fully conscious and aware of her situation, she was also able to give into panic, which she found herself doing with alarming quickness.

Swallowing her rising fear, she turned her head to look at her wrist and gave it an experimental tug. Though the rope chafed her skin, it didn't budge. If anything, it seemed to tighten around her wrist. Fighting the urge to scream in frustration, she yanked at her bonds again and again until her skin felt raw and she was breathing hard from fear as much as from exertion.

Flopping back on the bed, she stared up at the ceiling and blinked back tears. Who had kidnapped her, and what did they want? Had she stumbled onto someone doing something they shouldn't in the same way that she'd stumbled onto Kendall and his stripped books? Or did it have to do with the murders? She made a mental list of everyone she'd talked to that day, wondering who could have grabbed her, but she couldn't come up with anyone.

Just then, she heard voice coming from somewhere in the house. They were too soft and indistinct for her to hear what was being said, but as they drew closer, she realized that one of them was a woman.

Her heart pounding in her chest, Samantha tugged wildly at the ropes that secured her wrists to the bedposts, but to no avail.

Helpless to do anything but lie there and wait for the bedroom door to open, her eyes went wide when she saw the identity of her kidnappers.

David and Miranda Capshaw!

"You! But why...?" she gasped. All at once, realization began to dawn on her as she looked from David Capshaw to his wife. "You murdered Rick Elliot and Jeffrey Bauer, didn't you? But why? What could they have done to you? How could you even do something so…so…"

David Capshaw walked into the room to come stand beside the bed. He stood gazing down at her, a smug smile on his face, and it was all she could do not to squirm.

"Wrong?" he asked.

She glared up at him. "I was going to say horrible."

He regarded her thoughtfully for a moment. "Is it really that horrible? People kill each other all the time. Police, soldiers. Of course, in those cases, we've decided that doing something wrong is right if it's done for the proper reasons. We're simply playing word games with the rules that we ourselves have written. If we accept that our notion of murder comes with a long string of conditions, then is it really that wrong for Miranda and me to kill someone? It's nothing more than expressing just another exception to the rule."

Samantha stared at him in confusion. She had no idea what he was even talking about. "You're insane!" she cried.

He chuckled. "Insane? Well, there again, we have just another example of society writing arbitrary standards. But I doubt you would want to hear my opinions on that, since you're obviously already decided on the subject. Besides, it doesn't really matter. You couldn't understand why we do what we do, not in a million years." He glanced at his wife, who was leaning against the doorjamb, watching them. "The most important thing to understand is that killing those men made both Miranda and me very happy. Actually, to be truthful, murder gets Miranda incredibly hot."

Samantha felt like she was in an episode of the *Twilight Zone*. Only this wasn't some television show. The Capshaws were killers and she was at their mercy. She swallowed hard as Miranda Capshaw walked over to stand beside her husband.

"You can't really think you're going to get away with this," she said in a trembling voice.

Again, he smiled that smug smile. "Of course we do," he told her. "After all, we've been doing it for years and have never gotten caught."

Her brow furrowed. "I never heard of any murders at the university before this."

"Not this university, but others."

As he spoke, he trailed his fingers up her bare leg. She jerked, trying to pull away, but the rope around her ankle kept her firmly in place while his hand moved higher, pushing up her skirt, and she had to bite her lip to keep from screaming.

"You should feel honored, you know," he said conversationally. "I've never killed a woman before."

Samantha suddenly felt as if she had to struggle to breathe. Hearing him say the words seemed to make what was about to happen to her that much more horrifying.

"Dr. Capshaw..." she began. He was a college professor, an intelligent man. Surely, she could reason with him, she thought. "You don't have to kill me. I won't tell anyone anything."

He snorted. "That's why we brought you here, to make sure that you don't."

"You and your wife can disappear, and no one will ever know that you did it," she said desperately.

His mouth curved. "That's the plan."

She swallowed hard. If she couldn't reason with David Capshaw, she thought, then perhaps she could threaten him. "My boyfriend is one of the detectives working the case. I was talking to him when you grabbed me. He'll know that something's happened to me, and he'll come looking for me."

"No doubt," he agreed. "But by then, it'll be too late."

He ran his hand up her leg all the way to edge of her panties, and Samantha stiffened, watching in horror as his wife leaned in and covered his hand with her own, following where he led. Samantha began to struggle as much as the ropes would allow, but that only seemed to excite them even more. Just when she opened her mouth to scream, Miranda Capshaw grabbed her husband's chin and turned his face to hers and kissed him. Her mouth close to his ear, she whispered something that Samantha couldn't hear. He listened for a moment before starting to shake his head, but after a moment, he grinned and allowed his wife to lead him from the room.

Samantha fell back against the bed with a sigh of relief. She didn't know what Miranda Capshaw had said to her husband to get him to leave the room with her, and she didn't much care. She was just glad that they had.

She dragged in a deep breath, and then took another. Hayden would come for her. Knowing the knack she had for getting herself into trouble, he had to have realized that was exactly what had happened. But would he be able to figure out that the Capshaws were the ones who had kidnapped her? Would he know where they had taken her? More importantly, would he get to her in time?

Tears welling in her eyes, Samantha once again tugged at the ropes that bound her to the bed.

The tactical support unit arrived at the Capshaw address just as Hayden and his partner did. Men with automatic weapons and body armor jumped out of the back of the van and followed Hayden and Nik.

Hayden frowned. "What the...?" He began to get a sinking feeling. This couldn't be right. They weren't even in a residential section of town. It was more like a strip mall.

He quickly double-checked the address they'd gotten from the college administration, sure they must have been mistaken. The address was correct, but there was no house. The sign over the door read Home Mail, Inc.

He gestured for the other cops to remain where they were while he and Nik went into the building. There was a counter with what looked like hundreds of P.O. boxes behind it.

"Damn," he muttered. "It's some kind of mailing service."

The dark-haired girl behind the counter smiled at them. She was a teenager, probably a junior or senior in high school, and her nameplate said her name was Jennifer. "Can I help you?"

Hayden flashed his badge at her, but didn't bother introducing himself or his partner. "Is this address for one of your boxes?"

She glanced at the paper in his hand before nodding. "Yes."

"I need to know who it's registered to."

She hesitated. "Um...I'm not sure if I can give out that information without my supervisor's permission. I don't want to get in trouble."

Hayden clenched his jaw. "Look, I could get a warrant, but I don't have the time. Whoever owns this box has already murdered two people, and kidnapped another. Now, give me the damn name before I arrest you for refusing to cooperate with a police investigation."

The girl paled, looking nervously from him to Nik, before she turned to her computer. While she typed, Hayden saw his partner glance at him, but he ignored the look. His only concern was Samantha.

"Um...the box is registered to David and Miranda Capshaw," the girl said after a moment.

"Do you have an address on them?" Hayden asked.

She looked confused for a moment. "This is their address."

Hayden opened his mouth to snap at the girl, but Nik spoke before he could do so.

"We're looking for their actual physical address," he told her.

She smiled. "Oh, yes, here it is. It's 1214 Commerce Street."

Hayden swore under his breath as he recognized the address.

"That's the address for the damn police station," Nik said.

The girl shrugged. "Sorry, that's all I have. I didn't know."

"Then we need to get a look at their mail," Hayden said.

Again, Jennifer hesitated, but his scowl had her hurrying into the back. She came out almost immediately.

"They must have gotten their mail already," she said quietly.

Hayden swore again and started for the door, but Nik caught his arm before he could open it.

"We'll find her, Hayden," he said.

Hayden swallowed hard. "Before it's too late?"

Nik didn't answer.

Chapter Seven

"Okay, we've got the names of faculty these professors work with and the students they've had."

As he spoke, Conner handed out copies to the dozen or so detectives who were now working the case with Hayden and Nik. "Maybe the Capshaws had a party at their house. Maybe a student stopped by their house to get some papers. Whatever. There has to be someone who knows where these people actually live."

Hayden stared at the list that Conner had given him. Even with the additional help, it would take hours to track down all these people, and by then, Samantha could be... He clamped down hard on the thought, refusing to give voice to his fear. Clenching his jaw, he reached for the phone on his desk.

"You know, if we do get a lead in these people, I'm thinking that maybe you should sit this one out, Hayden."

He looked up at the sound of Nik's voice, his brow furrowing. "What?"

"I'm just saying that you're too close to this. You obviously have feelings for Samantha, and that could cloud your judgment. This isn't the time to be making bad decisions."

Nik was careful to keep his voice low, Hayden was relieved to see. Conner didn't know about Hayden's relationship with Samantha, but if he did, he'd almost surely pull him off the case, for precisely the reason that Nik had pointed out.

"What would you do if it were Krista, Nik?" Hayden demanded, his voice just as soft. "Would you be content to sit here and twiddle your thumbs while the woman you love is at the mercy of some psychopath?"

The words were out before he realized he'd said them. He noticed that Nik didn't seem surprised at all to hear him say it, even though he certainly was. Could it really be possible? Was he in love with Samantha? After only a week? It sounded crazy. But now that it was out there, it felt right somehow. Now all he had to do was find Samantha and see if she felt the same way.

But reaching this conclusion about his feelings for Samantha did nothing to calm him, and Nik could see that. His partner leaned in close.

"I'll let you make the call, because that's the way I'd want it," he said. "Just remember, I'm your partner. Don't go doing anything stupid without letting me know first." He paused long enough to look at the paper that Conner had handed out. "Let's get to work on these names. I'll start at the bottom and you start at the top, okay?"

Hayden didn't trust his voice, so he just nodded. He noticed his hand was trembling as he reached for the phone and put it to his ear, then dialed the number of the first person on his list, Brian Jones.

But Brian Jones couldn't give him any information about the Capshaws. Nor could Janine Colby, Marianne Hall, Lawrence McKenzie, or anyone else on the list that he was able to reach. What he was left with were about a dozen names for people who were either no longer at the phone number listed, or hadn't answered the phone altogether.

Nik and the other detectives were still working the phones, but the few who had finished were starting a list on the board at the front of the room of those people they hadn't been able to reach. Remarks to the side of each name were added: moved out of state, not at home, and in one case, no longer living. Hayden added his names to the growing list.

Two detectives had already started looking up addresses for those that weren't living with their parents anymore. The ones that had moved out of the area would be a lot tougher to track down.

Hayden poured a cup of coffee and tried to stay calm, but it was no good. He needed to do something or he was going to go crazy. Grabbing up the first list of addresses that came out of the printer, he gave Conner a nod.

"I'll get started running down these names," he said. "If they can't help, you can give me more addresses."

Conner must have thought it was a good idea because he simply motioned with his hand for Hayden to get going.

Nik, who had just finished with his list, stepped in front of him. "I'll go with you."

Hayden glanced at him. "We can work faster if we both take some," he said, handing his partner half. "I'll call if I get anything."

"Make sure you do," Nik said quietly. "Don't go off trying to do this by yourself."

"I won't," Hayden assured him. "I'll call."

With that, he was out the door and headed toward the apartment of one of the recent college graduates. When the girl didn't answer the door, he knocked on her neighbor's, an elderly woman who gave him the girl's work address. But tracking her down turned out to be a waste of time, as did talking to the next several people, all of whom had no idea where the Capshaws lived, and by the time Hayden got to the apartment of a recent grad named James Williams, he was thoroughly frustrated and half out of his mind with worry. This was taking way too long, and anything could have happened to Samantha by now.

He told himself to wait patiently after he rang the doorbell, but when no one answered, he found himself knocking repeatedly until someone did. The pretty girl that yanked the door open looked like she wanted to bite off his head, but one look at his badge and she bit back whatever it was she'd been about to say.

"I'm looking for James Williams," he said.

She looked taken aback. "Is he in some kind of trouble?"

He shook his head. "I need to talk to him about a professor he had in college." He glanced over her shoulder and into the living room impatiently. "Is he here?"

"Actually, he's at the gym," she said. "But I can tell him that you came by, if you want."

He shook his head again. "I need to talk to him right away. What gym does he work out at?"

"At the health club around the corner."

Hayden quickly thanked her and left. A few minutes later, he was flashing his badge at the front desk of the health club and asking for James Williams.

The girl looked at the desk looked at him curiously for a moment, and then pointed out a tall, blond guy jogging on a treadmill.

Hayden walked over to him. "James Williams?"

The man glanced at the badge he held. "Yeah," he said, continuing to jog.

"I'm Detective Tanner. I need to ask you about a professor you had in college. Miranda Capshaw."

James said nothing for a moment, but then he slowed the treadmill to a walk before stepping off the machine. Grabbing the towel from the handrail, he wiped his hands.

"What about her?" he asked.

"It's extremely important that I talk to her," Hayden told him. "The address she listed at the college is fake and I'm hoping you might know where she and her husband actually live?"

James was silent for a moment before he nodded. "Yeah, I know where she lives," he said. "She invited me over once. She wanted to sleep with me, but I backed out after I got there. It was just a little bit too weird for me. I kept thinking her husband was lurking in the closet waiting for us to get it on or something. She was hot looking, but that's not my thing. I made up some excuse and got the hell out of there."

Hayden felt his pulse race. "Do you know the address?"

"No, but I can give you directions."

Hayden pulled out his notebook and began to write them down. As he did, he realized that the Capshaws lived well outside of town and that it would take him at least thirty minutes to get there.

Taking out his cell phone, he dialed Conner's number as he got in the car.

"It's Tanner. I've got directions to the Capshaw's house," he said when the man answered, and then proceeded to fill Conner in on what he'd learned. "I'm on my way there now."

"Good work. I'll have tactical support meet you, but don't go in until they get there," Conner said.

Hayden said nothing, but his hand tightened on the wheel as he drove. He knew his first instinct would be to kick in the door and charge into the house, but Conner was right. He needed to wait for back up...if he could.

When he got to the Capshaw's place, a big two-story house set way back in the woods, he pulled off the road and hid the car in the trees. He knew he should stay in the car, but he couldn't. So instead, he headed through the woods toward the side of the house. He had every intention of waiting there until his back up arrived, but then he heard the scream.

Samantha. He couldn't wait any longer. Swearing under his breath, he pulled his gun free of its holster and raced toward the house.

Samantha stared up at the ceiling and tried hard to fight back the tears that welled in her eyes. She'd done everything she could think of to get free of the ropes binding her to the bed, but no matter how hard she'd jerked on them, or how gently she'd wiggled her wrists, nothing had worked. And all the while, she'd had to listen to David and Miranda Capshaw having sex in the next room.

She closed her eyes, shutting out the sounds her kidnappers were making, and thought of Hayden. She almost smiled as she remembered thinking how arrogant and obnoxious he was that day she'd met him in the bookstore. But the Hayden she knew now was kind and warm and loving, and just the type of man she had always imagined herself falling in love with. She just hoped she had the chance to tell him how she felt about him.

The sound of the door opening jerked her from her thoughts, and she stiffened as the Capshaws came into the room. They were there to finish what they'd started earlier; she could see it in their eyes. She was never going to see Hayden again, she realized. A tear slowly trickled down her cheek and she turned her face away, not wanting them to see it.

But David Capshaw didn't seem to notice, not even when he gripped her chin and forced her to look at him.

"So, Ms. Halliwell, while I was otherwise occupied, a thought occurred to me," he said, his voice soft, but his eyes coldly assessing her. "Did you tell anyone about us?"

She was taken aback by the question for a moment. "I told you," she said shakily. Her mind raced, trying to think of something to say that would change their mind about killing her. "My boyfriend's a detective. In fact, it was his idea that I talk to your wife. He had his suspicions that your wife might be involved, since she knew both of the students. Everything pointed to you as the jealous husband. He thought that your wife would open up to me since I'm a woman. He thoughts I could trick her into incriminating herself. Or you."

David Capshaw's eyes narrowed, but then he chuckled. "You're good, I'll give you that, but you're lying. Cops don't work with reporters, not even when they're sleeping with them. And even if you were, what cop is going to let his woman do his investigating for him?" He paused. "But again, it was a good try."

As he spoke, he trailed his hand down her neck to follow the V of her shirt. But before Samantha could do more than open her mouth to protest, Miranda Capshaw's sharp voice cut in.

"David!"

He ignored his wife to run his hand over Samantha's breast and down her stomach, making her stiffen.

"David, we agreed!" Miranda Capshaw's voice rose and she took a step closer. "You said that you wouldn't touch her."

He tossed his wife an impatient glance over his shoulder, his mouth tightening. "I've watched you touch other men for years, Miranda."

She said nothing for a moment, then her brow furrowed. "But I did that for you, David."

98

He smirked. "How selfless. You enjoyed it as much as I did. Probably more."

She shook her head. "No, no that's not true. I did it only because you wanted me to."

David Capshaw left Samantha to walk over to where his wife stood by the door. "Miranda, this could be a whole new dimension for us," he said, lifting her chin. "You could even find that you enjoy it."

"David, I..."

But he silenced her with a kiss, and when he lifted his head, she nodded, clearly acquiescing. Saying something to his wife that Samantha couldn't hear, David Capshaw turned and walked back to the bed.

Samantha tried to tell herself that if she could just keep him talking, it would give Hayden time to find her, but her mind, usually so clever and resourceful, was a complete blank now, and when David Capshaw put his hands on her, all she could do was scream.

Laughing at her desperate cries for help, David Capshaw bent over her, yanking at her shirt. She screamed again, louder this time, twisting and struggling as much as the ropes would allow. Anything to keep him from getting her clothes off. Then, abruptly, he tensed, cocking his head to the side as if listening to something.

Samantha held her breath, wondering what had caught his attention. Then she heard it. A noise downstairs, like someone had kicked in the front door.

Relief coursing through her, she opened her mouth to scream, but David Capshaw clamped his hand tightly over her mouth, muffling the sound.

"It's the police!" Miranda Capshaw said from her place in the doorway. "David, leave her and let's go!"

He stared down at Samantha, indecision clearly written on his face, and for a moment she thought that despite the police banging down his door, he would actually still try to rape her before making his escape. Swearing under his breath, he reached out and grabbed something off the bedside table. A moment later, he took his hand away from her mouth, replacing it with a piece of cloth. Tying it tightly behind her head, he gave her one last look, then he hurried out the door with his wife, leaving Samantha alone in the room.

Fear for Samantha had his adrenalin pumping so hard that Hayden could barely hear over the pounding of his own heart as he entered the house. His gun poised, he quickly scanned the downstairs. He had a clear view of the living and dining rooms, and a bit of the kitchen as well, but he saw no one. Indecision gripped him for a moment. The house was so large that it would take forever to clear every room. He closed his eyes for just a second and tried to imagine where he had heard the screams coming from. It had definitely been from upstairs. Thoughts of a more thorough check of the ground floor fled his mind and he immediately headed for the stairs.

He knew he was moving way too fast, that someone could be hiding anywhere and he'd never see them. But the screaming had stopped and the silence scared him even more than the screams had.

Reaching the top of the landing, he made his way down the hallway. The first room he came to was empty, though the bed looked like it had been recently slept in. When he didn't see Samantha, he quickly moved on to the next. Pushing open the door, he almost sagged against the doorframe with relief when he saw Samantha lying on the bed, bound and gagged.

She was looking at him wide-eyed and tearful, and the emotions that rushed through him were almost overwhelming. Concerns about where the hell the Capshaws were and making sure that Samantha hadn't been hurt warred inside him.

He glanced quickly around the room. There was a closet against one wall, but the doors were wide open, and he could see that there was no one hiding in it. Rushing over to the bed, he pulled the gag from Samantha's mouth, and then went to work o the ropes binding her to the bed.

"Hayden..." she whispered through her tears. "I can't believe you found me."

100

The knots were tighter than they looked and he had to put the gun down on the bed to work on them with both hands. He swore under his breath when he saw how red and chafed her skin was. It was even bleeding a little. "Did they hurt you?"

She shook her head from side to side on the pillow. "No...no, they were going to, but then they heard you. They just left a minute before you came in the door. I...I don't know where they went."

He yanked at the knots, working them loose. "I've got back-up coming. Samantha, you need to..."

But she didn't let him finish. "Hayden, listen to me. They murdered Rick Elliot and..."

Her words ended in a scream, but before he even realized what was happening, a man's hands closed over his throat. Instinctively, he went for his gun, but his attacker jerked him backward just as he grabbed for it and the weapon fell off the bed and out of his reach.

Hayden felt the edges of his vision start to go dark. Shit. He had to get Capshaw off him before he passed out. But trying to pull at the man's hands wasn't working, so he brought his arm forward and jabbed his elbow into David Capshaw's gut. The man let out a grunt, but didn't release his grip on him. Hayden repeated the move over and over, driving his elbow repeatedly into the man's stomach and chest.

Finally, Capshaw fell backward, releasing him. Hayden dragged in a grateful breath before going for his gun. But Capshaw reached for it at the same time and the weapon went sliding across the wood floor as they both grappled to get their hands on it.

Samantha had one foot free and was untying the ropes on the other when she heard the gun go off. Her heart suddenly in her throat, she jerked her head around to see Hayden and David Capshaw locked together. Neither man moved and she looked from one to the other, wondering which one had been shot and desperately hoping it hadn't been Hayden.

Then, after what seemed like ages, David Capshaw rolled over onto his back and was still. His hands were clutched to his chest where she could see a bloodstain spreading.

Hayden was still kneeling on the floor, the gun at his side, his breathing ragged. Samantha scrambled off the bed and rushed into his arms. He held her tightly, his cheek pressed against the top of her head. For the first time since she'd been kidnapped, she felt like she could finally breathe.

"I thought I'd never see you again," she sobbed against his chest. "I never thought you'd find me."

Hayden lifted her chin and gently pressed a finger to her lips. "Samantha, I love you," he said softly. "I would have found you no matter where they'd taken you."

She stared up at him for a moment, too surprised by the words to do more than that, but before she could tell him that she was in love with him, too, a commotion at the door interrupted them. She turned to see Hayden's partner coming into the room, along with several other cops. They all had their guns drawn, but lowered them when they saw that both she and Hayden were safe.

Nik glanced at Capshaw's body. "You okay?" he asked, looking at Hayden.

Hayden nodded. "Yeah," he said. "Miranda Capshaw took off, though."

"We got her. She was outside." Nik glanced at the body on the floor. "I thought I said something about not trying to do this on your own."

Hayden shrugged, but said nothing, and after a moment his partner gave him a nod and walked over to talk to the other cops as they moved into the room. One of them bent down to check David Capshaw for a pulse. He came up shaking his head. Samantha shivered.

"Come on," Hayden said. "Let's get you out of here."

Samantha said nothing as he slipped an arm around her waist and led her out of the room. Once in the hallway, however, she stopped. He turned to face her.

"What is it?" he asked, his dark eyes full of concern.

"I just wanted to thank you," she said softly, then stood up on tiptoe to kiss him gently on the mouth. "And tell you that I love you, too."

Samantha's story about the Capshaws had run in the next day's edition of the Post. Though her editor had gruffly told her that she was supposed to report the news, not make it, he'd been so pleased with her work that he took her out of the arts and leisure section and put her in the newsroom full time, much to her delight.

To her surprise, the kidnapping had made her something of a celebrity in Seattle. She'd been asked to do several interviews with other papers, as well as a few magazines, and had even been a guest on a local television talk show. She would also have to testify against Miranda Capshaw at the woman's trial, of course. The psychology professor was claiming that her husband had forced her to take part in the murders, and since David Capshaw couldn't deny it, Samantha intended to make sure that the truth came out.

Hayden had also taken Samantha out on a "real" date, which was kind of amusing in a way, considering that they had not only slept together already, but had admitted their love as well. The date, however, was wonderful. They'd gone to dinner and a movie, and then come back to her place, where they'd just finished making love. She had been waiting for Hayden to take her to task for getting herself kidnapped, but he hadn't so much as mentioned a spanking. She supposed he figured that after what had happened, she'd learned her lesson.

As they lay entwined together, her head on his shoulder, she ran her fingers down his naked chest. "My editor liked my story so much that he put me in the newsroom permanently," she said quietly, pushing herself up on an elbow to look at him. "Are you okay with that?"

He regarded her thoughtfully. "That depends."

"On?"

His mouth quirked. "On whether you're going to get yourself into trouble every time you work on a story."

She shrugged. "That depends."

"On?"

Her mouth curved. "On whether you're going to spank me every time I get myself into trouble."

He lifted a brow.

"You know, you don't have to wait for me to get myself into trouble before you spank me," she continued.

His brow went even higher. "Really?"

She shrugged and looked away, suddenly shy. "You could spank me...well...just because..."

He put his fingers under her chin and gently turned her face back to his. "Are you asking me to spank you, Samantha?"

Blushing, she nodded.

Hayden gently kissed her. "Get your hairbrush, Samantha," he said softly.

She pulled back to look at him, her beautiful, blue eyes full of surprise. "My hairbrush?"

He ran his finger down her cheek. "Mmm. I noticed it when you were brushing your hair. It's the perfect size for spanking, and with all that beautiful, polished wood, it's guaranteed to make that cute, little bottom of yours very red."

She felt her pulse quicken. "Hayden..."

He kissed her, slowly. "The hairbrush, Samantha."

His soft voice made her powerless to do anything but obey, and she got off the bed to pad naked into the bathroom. When she came back in, she saw that Hayden was sitting up against the headboard, a pillow draped across his thigh.

Samantha felt her pulse skip a beat, and her hand tightened on the handle of the brush. Despite the fact that the hairbrush would probably smart more than Hayden's hand ever could, her body was tingling with the anticipation of being spanked with it.

"Come here, Samantha," Hayden said softly, patting the bed with his hand.

Fingering the hairbrush nervously, she slowly walked across the room to climb onto the bed.

"Not too hard, though, okay?" she said, offering him the hairbrush.

He kissed her, gently tugging on her lower lip. "Not harder than you can take, love."

Taking the hairbrush, he gently guided her over his knee, and then held her in place with his hand once she was comfortably situated on the pillow.

Samantha held her breath, waiting to feel the slap of the hairbrush, but what she felt instead was Hayden's warm hand as he slowly caressed her bare skin, and she let out a little sigh of pleasure. What was it about being draped over her lover's knee for a spanking that got her so excited? Was it the knowledge that she was giving up control? Was it the secret desire she had to be a "bad girl?" Or was it that she simply enjoyed having her bottom turned a glowing shade of red because it felt so darn good?

SMACK!

She gasped as he brought his hand down. "*Oh!*"

He laughed softly. "I haven't even started yet, love," he chastised her.

She squirmed against him and he spanked her again, more forcefully this time, following it up with another and another until her bottom was stinging, and she was squirming so much that he had to put his free leg over hers to keep her in place.

Not that Hayden didn't enjoy her wiggling. In fact, it was all he could do not to pull her on top of him and plunge himself deep inside her. He stopped spanking her to trail his hand over the curve of her asscheeks. Slipping his hand between her legs, he gently ran his finger along the slick folds to her clit. She moaned as he made little circular motions with his finger, and then whimpered when he drew his hand away. As much as he loved touching her, he still had the hairbrush to use on her, he reminded himself. Though he had to admit, knowing how hot and wet she already was had him testing the limits of his control.

Reaching for the hairbrush, he gently caressed her reddened bottom with the highly polished back.

Samantha let out a little moan of pleasure. Which quickly turned into a yelp of surprise as Hayden brought the hairbrush down sharply on her sore bottom.

"*Owww!*"

He spanked her again, ignoring her protests, and she gripped the pillow tightly as he smacked the brush against her right cheek, then her left, and then her right, again and again.

"*Owww!* Hayden, that stings!" she whined, squirming against the pillow.

The corner of his mouth quirked. "That's the idea." Unable to resist, he placed his hand on her well-spanked bottom, and was rewarded with a moan from Samantha. "Your ass looks so good red," he said huskily.

As he spoke, Hayden lifted his knee a little so that her reddened bottom was even higher. He felt her tense, and knew she was waiting for him to spank her. Instead, he bent his head to press his lips to her red-hot skin.

Samantha moaned as he trailed kisses over her hot and stinging bottom.

"Hayden...please..." she breathed.

"Please, what?" he asked, kissing her ass again.

She pushed herself up and turned around to straddle his lap. "Never mind," she said. "If you can't figure out what I need, I'll take care of it myself."

Hayden chuckled as she sank down on his hard cock.

"That was incredible," Samantha said as she snuggled against his chest afterward.

Spent, Hayden couldn't do more than mumble something unintelligible in agreement.

Beside the bed, his cell phone rang. He swore silently. Reaching for it, he flipped it open and brought it to his ear. "Tanner."

106

He listened for a moment, and then sighed. "Yeah. I'll be there in twenty minutes."

Hanging up, he pulled Samantha close and kissed the top of her head. "I gotta go. They found a body in a dumpster behind the Piedmont Hotel."

She sat up, watching as he got out of bed, and then did the same herself.

"I'll tag along," she told him, reaching for her clothes.

He paused in the act of buttoning his jeans to give her a stern look. "Just behave yourself."

Her lips curved. "What are you going to do if I don't, Detective?" she asked sweetly. "Spank me?"

As he watched her sexy ass disappear into the bathroom, Hayden found himself hoping that Samantha wouldn't behave herself at all.

Blushing Books ® hopes you enjoyed this spicy, spanking novel by Joannie Kay. We have lots of other erotic novels and novellas available. For the "latest," you may want to check out our Internet websites, owned and operated by our Internet partner, ABCD Webmasters.

Bethany's Woodshed has been publishing erotic and romantic spanking novels since 1998. Each week the website is updated with six new novels or short stories, featuring adult romantic and erotic spanking stories. Every story published on Bethany's Woodshed is original, exclusive, brand- new, and all are written by paid professionals. Bethany's Woodshed is located at: http://www.herwoodshed.com

Spanking Romance is also a site which is updated weekly. At this site, we publish a completed novella – 4-6 chapters – every week. Again, all stories are brand new and exclusive, written by paid professionals.
Spanking Romance is located at: http://www.spankingromance.com

Romantic Spankings is our eBook site. On this site there are literally hundreds of eBook novels and novellas, all available for immediate download.
Romantic Spankings is located at: http://www.romanticspankings.com

Many of our longer books are also available in print through Amazon. Please check out the following titles:

A Glitch in Time by Judith McClaren ISBN: 978-1-935152-00-2
Master of Wyndham Hall by Sullivan Clarke ISBN: 978-1-935152-01-9
Barbarian Worlds by Sharon Green ISBN: 978-1-935152-02-5
Cindra and The Bounty Hunter by Paige Tyler ISBN: 978-1-935152-03-3
Victorian Brats Volume One by Melinda Barron ISBN: 978-1-935152-04-0
Princess Brat by Sharon Green ISBN: 978-1-935152-05-7
Mistaken by Laurel Joseph ISBN: 978-1-935152-06-4
Magic Spell by Paige Tyler ISBN: 978-1-935152-07-1
The Cutler Brothers by Paige Tyler ISBN: 978-1-935152-08-8
Simple Pleasures by Nattie Jones ISBN: 978-1-935152-09-5
DeAkeny's Bride by Darla Phelps: ISBN: 978-1-935152-10-1
The Friends Series, Volume One by Paige Tyler: ISBN 978-1-935152-11-8
Comanche Canyon, by Judith McClaren: ISBN 978-1-935152-12-5
Second Chances by Carolyn Faulkner: ISBN 978-1-935152-13-2
If You Loved Me by Starla Kaye: ISBN 978-1-935152-14-9

The New Panty Collection by Joannie Kaye: ISBN 978-1-935152-15-6
Last Chance by Joannie Kaye: ISBN 978-1-935152-16-3
Kayla and The Rancher by Paige Tyler: ISBN 978-1-935152-17-0
Samantha and the Detective by Paige Tyler: ISBN 978-1-935152-18-7

2017667